UnOrThodox

STEPHANIE DESCHENES

unorthodox

By

Stephanie Deschenes

Visit our website at **www.StillwaterPress.com** for more information.

First Stillwater River Publications Edition

ISBN-10: 0-692-64942-5
ISBN-13: 978-0692-64942-8
Library of Congress Control Number: 2016939138
1 2 3 4 5 6 7 8 9 10
Written by Stephanie Deschenes
Cover Design by Dawn M. Porter
Published by Stillwater River Publications, Glocester, RI, USA.

I dedicate this book to

– Oh boy –

My parents, my brother Brandon, my "sibling" Emma Fague, my Aunt Aline Uth and Uncle Cham, my best friends Elizabeth Greenleaf and Crystal Pace. I don't know what I would do without you guys.

Dad, thank you for being a superhero. Mother, thank you for making me who I am today. Bran, thank you for being the golden child. Auntie and Uncle Cham thank you for being my second set of parents. Memeré, thank you for being the inspiringly kind woman you are. Aunt Terri and Uncle Sodan, thank you for opening my eye to things I wouldn't have otherwise.

Along with another thanks to Sydnie Weston, Tracey Weston, Danielle Merrill, Brenda, Greg and Sydney Duquette, and Abigail Chadwick. I might have turned out different without the influence you all provided.

I am very grateful.

Unorthodox:
contrary to what is usual, traditional,
or accepted.

1.

Physique

Come on, reach! It's just a couple inches. If I try jumping to it again, I'm just gonna fall and smash into the wall. I'm not releasing my feet from these footholds until I have a firm grip on *that* rock. Just a little further. My fingers slide over the side of the plastic. I need a grip. I push myself up further with my toes. Come on, please. Please. Fuck it, I'm gonna jump for it. I retreat slightly to coil my feet for lift off. I breathe in, out. I grab the handhold tighter and yank as I shoot myself upward. Joy washes over me as I feel the top of *that* rock. I tighten my grip and hold on. Yes. I got it. I fucking got it. I clutch the rock like it's life itself and lift my foot to the new foothold that will provide the leverage I need to touch the last rock at the top.

I've been working on this wall all week; it's the hardest one in the building. Rock climbing came pretty easy to me, just like every other physical endeavor I've ever taken up. I only started rock climbing in the middle of last week, and now I smack the top rock with my palm with a victorious feeling in my gut I've graduated. HA! And it's only... I twist my arm away from my goal and look at my watch. Fuck! Shit, shit, shit! I was supposed to be at the range twenty-three minutes ago! Fuck! Max is going to fucking kill me.

I push off and let the auto belay bring me to a lower part of the wall where I kick off a couple of times 'til I'm back on the ground. Quickly, I unclasp myself and attach the leash to the clip on the bottom of the wall.

Fuck my life! How did the time go by that fast? I was totally on top of it! How is it that this always happens? I run to the cubbie and grab my things then fall back on the raised bouldering mat to change from the rental shoes into my sneakers.

"You made it!" The guy at the front desk calls over as he makes a single movement to jump over the desk, to sit on it and dangle his feet over the front.

I finish sliding my second shoe on, stand up, and step out of my harness.

"You've been watching me?" I cock my eyebrow.

"Hope you don't mind."

I bend to pick up my bag, sling it around my shoulder and grab the rentals.

"Hey, whatever man." I walk up and place the shoes and harness beside him. "I gotta run."

"You climb outside the gym?" He nudges his chin at me.

"Not yet."

"I've seen a lot a pros struggle for weeks on that beast you just destroyed. I go out climbing with a bunch of people every Sunday. You should come with us."

"I'll let 'cha know," I smile.

"Rad, I'll *hold* you to that."

"I gotta go."

"See you around."

I give him one last smile and push through the glass door to the parking lot.

I rummage through my bag for keys as I run to my car, locating them relatively quickly. I shove the key into the door. The battery in the key died a while back so I can't unlock it with the button anymore. Flinging the door open, I plant my butt on the seat and close myself in. S'not *that* bad... I mean... I've been *later*. This is nothing. I twist the key in the ignition and the car makes a sound like it *wants* to start, but it doesn't. Shit! Why won't the engine turn over? I try it again. Same. Again. Same.

Oh, fuck this shit! I get out of the car and slam the door. The range isn't far, I'll run there. It'll take me fifteen minutes tops. Faster than trying to get this piece of shit running. Plus, I'll get a good run out of it....

"Ah! So the queen arrives!" Max bellows with thick sarcasm.

"Sorry, Max," I keep my voice small.

I hate putting myself in a situation where I have to bite my tongue and let people yell at me. I know I'm in the wrong. I know. But I still have to be extra vigilant to make sure I don't defend myself. *You deserve this. Just be cool.*

"If your dad hadn't taken a bullet for me – "

"I know, I know.

That bullet has gotten me out of an astounding amount of shit. Max is my dad's best friend. They were in the army together and they go back to childhood. Ever since I was little, he's been like a second father to me. Collectively, I have probably spent a little over three years of my life living at his place when I needed a break from sharing a house with my mother. I have my own room over there that will always be waiting for me, no matter how late I come into work or how badly I piss him off.

"Any particular reason for today's delay?"

"Actually yes," I perk up. Yes! I can say I wasn't late *before* the car broke down. He doesn't have to know that I was already twenty-five minutes late before I found out my car wouldn't start. "I had to walk from the rock gym; my car's busted."

I take my place behind the desk and look at the check-in book. We're full. Great, it's been busy. This makes me look even worse.

"Sophie Fileux! You went through *that* part of town on foot? Kid, that's a bad area, come on! I know it's hard. I know caution is not your thing. But can you just try being safe? Just once in a while? You know, to shake things up?"

"I'm not afraid of people, Max. It's fine. I made it here, didn't I?

"You sound just like your father. I *know* you're not afraid, that's what *scares me*. You're gonna get yourself shot someday."

"With this face?" I joke, circling my finger around my face for emphasis. "Yeah right," I smirk.

He smiles.

"You got a smart mouth, you know that? *That* and your *face* are not going help you if you're walking through a back alley. I really wish you would use your brain."

"Would you stop worrying about me? Please? I can handle myself."

He shakes his head and retires to the office.

* * *

"So what do you mean your car's busted?"

I place the last weapon of my shift in its designated spot and turn to look at him.

"Won't start. I don't know why."

"Ken will be here in about five minutes, as long he isn't anything like you. I'm gonna give you a ride."

"No, it's alright Max. I'm just gonna run back and call a tow truck."

"No. It's dark out. I'm driving you home and you can tell the big tow truck men where they can find your car."

I sigh. There's no use arguing.

"Alright, fine," I shrug and let my arms fall and hand slap the sides of my legs.

"So."

I stop staring out the passenger window to give him my full attention. This is usually how he starts a heavy topic. This should be good.

"Have you heard from your mother yet?"

"You say *yet*, like I'm *going to* eventually."

"Well I just thought... with Bruce off in Florida doing that summer program... she'd maybe check-in."

"Well *he's* the golden child, maybe she *did* check-in with *him*. I don't know."

"You and your brother are tight. If that were the case, he would have told you – you know that."

"I know, I know, I just… no, I haven't heard from her," I finish with a clipped tone that I wasn't shooting for. I was going more for indifferent.

"How's ya' dad?"

"I dunno Max, why don't you ask *him*?"

We're both quiet for a couple minutes.

"How are *you* doing?"

"I'm fine, Max. I'm always fine. I will *always be* fine. You don't have to keep asking me."

"Everyone's takin' off on you, kiddo. I worry about ya."

"They're not taking off on me, they just have places to be. I'll find somewhere to go too… someday. After I finish helping Dad dig his way out of the debt Ma left us. Stop worrying. You know I hate that."

2.

Nightmares

The endless white hallway seems even longer tonight. No matter how far I run, the end never comes any closer. In fact, I can't even *see* an end. It seems to extend before me, even though I'm already practically jogging in place. Where the white walls meet the equally white ceiling there are rows of blinding light bulbs stretching all the way down the hall for as far as I can see. Behind me, the bulbs crackle and pop, darkening the distance I've traveled. Desperate to stay ahead of the expanding blackness that is rapidly approaching me, I continue to run. I turn my head to catch a brief glance at the following obscurity. The quick peek costs me my coordination. Tripping over my own feet, I land in the arms of a blinding bright figure.

"You shouldn't have done that," He gently scolds, helping me to regain my balance in front of him. It was as if he was made from the contents of the light bulbs that hung on the ceiling. I squint my eyes in an attempt to make out some features. It's too bright, I have to close them.

"Done what?" I ask impatiently.

"It was the wrong decision. You need to think ahead, Sophie."

"But I don't know what to do."

"You need to figure it out," he states unimpressed, with a dry half-chuckle.

"I know!" I shout at him still clenching my eyelids together.

Suddenly, I feel hostile.

"Can't you see I'm trying? I don't know what to do! I need time! Just leave me alone!" I swing my arm to break his hold but it's already gone. I open my eyes and there is no bright figure.

I must have insulted him. I feel as though I've done something wrong and hate myself for it.

"I'm sorry!" I call out to him. "I'm trying!"

He was only trying to help, and I shouted at him. I'm such a horrible person. If I keep this up, I'll have no one left.

"I'm sorry!" I call again, louder than before.

I turn to look for him. I look into the darkness. I take a step towards it. No longer is it approaching me, now it's waiting, challenging me. I feel if I run, it will charge, so I hold my ground, staring it down.

"You *have* no time," the voice calls to me from the dark.

The next row of light bulbs starts to flicker, like a wolf baring its teeth and snarling in warning, Mohawk up. I take a step back without turning, then another. The next step brings my back to a hard surface. I turn to observe the obstruction. A wall. I'm trapped. I feel claustrophobic. I start hyperventilating. I return my gaze to the blackness and suddenly – everything is gone. It's pitch dark. I touch my fingertips to my brows and drape my hands over my eyes trying to at least see my fingers.

"Try harder."

I can't tell if the voice is extremely close or in my head.

Am I awake? I look around my bedroom. The dark gray walls emphasize the darkness that surrounds me. When did I wake up? I'm sitting up and everything. That was weird. I flop my hand around the wall beside my bed until I locate the light switch and flip it up. All of my covers are on the floor, and the fitted sheet is half torn off the mattress.

"Shit." I breathe.

What does the clock say? *2:34*. I get up and pull the fitted sheet completely off the bed so the stupid elastic won't get stuck between my feet while I'm trying to fall back asleep. I hate that. I grab the comforter out of the heap of blankets on the floor and pull it up with me as I dive back onto the bed.

3.

Priorities

An incoming call wakes me this time. I press the accept button on the screen and place the phone on top of my ear without even sitting up.

"Yeah?" I mumble.

"Are you still sleeping?"

By the sound of Dad's perturbed voice, it can't be any earlier than 10:00. I pull the phone away from my ear and hold it on the pillow in front of my eyes. *11:17.* Oh.

"No. Nope I'm up, I'm upstairs, I'm eating breakfast."

"When did you get up?" He asks skeptically.

"It's been at least a solid 20 minutes; it was definitely within the 10 o'clock hour."

He laughs lightly into the phone.

"The 10 o'clock hour?" He repeats.

"Yeah," I assure him.

"So 10:58 is still in the 10 o'clock hour?"

"Yeah, it makes it sound earlier to say it that way."

"I see," he laughs again. "Hey, can you make that vegetarian stew, you make that's really good, that takes like all day to cook?

"Yeah, OK."

He's got this thing with stew every once in a while and he knows I won't make it unless it's vegetarian.

"So you're gonna get up now?"

"Yup."

"Good. Get goin'."

"'Kay."

"Alright, I'll talk to later, love you."

"Love you."

He knew I was lying about being up, but he's always entertained by the way I can make anything sound acceptable. I sit up slowly and swing my feet off the bed to the floor.

Hmm, what takes priority over making this soup? As a procrastinator, I am compelled to determine what these potential tasks may be.

On the way to the kitchen, I stop at the bathroom to brush my teeth and get the awful morning breath taste out of my mouth. I grab my toothbrush and the toothpaste out of the cupboard and look into the mirror. My short dark brown hair, that falls about two inches above my shoulders, is sticking out in all directions on one side of my head, and is completely flat on the other side of my head. My dark brown eyes, that I can't keep completely open yet, have purplish bags underneath them, even though I got plenty of sleep.

It wasn't restful though. That was an odd dream last night. I prefer dreamless sleep to having dreams like that. What did it mean, that I don't know where I'm going with my life? I hate thinking about this. I don't know what I want to do, I really don't. I should be *doing* something by now, heading toward something at least… right? Or is this normal? The shooting range is great for now, but what's next for me? I can't stay there forever.

I brush my teeth for several minutes before deciding they're clean enough to eat something. Smoothing the crazy mop on my head with my fingers, I'm satisfied with my bathroom detour. I start down the hallway for the kitchen again.

I cross the kitchen and rest my head on the closed freezer door while I let the fridge door hang open so I can peer inside. No milk. That means cereal is out. Fuck — I love cereal. I close the fridge and move on to the cupboard. I see a box of crackers, pretzel sticks and an oatmeal container. Eh, I just grab the oats then a bowl and spoon out of the dishwasher.

I sit on the counter and wait, pulling out my phone to check my email while the microwave continues to hum. At a glance, I decide it's all junk mail – coupons I won't use. Opening my music, I put on some mild morning stuff and slide my phone into the back pocket of my pajama pants. The microwave beep sounds. I jump down from the counter to retrieve my breakfast.

Placing the bowl on the counter where I had been sitting, I open the fridge to find the stew meat. The oats need to cool for a second anyway.

* * *

Now that the stew is cooking and I've taken a shower, I'm gonna go for a run. But wait... first, I should go throw some knives at the tree out back. I haven't done it in a couple days; don't want to fall out of practice. I get to my room and drop my towel to the floor, before opening my underwear drawer. I pull on some under garments and open the next drawer down, grab a pair of running shorts, pulling them on as well. I finish the ensemble with a tank top and get my throwing knives from their resting place in the basket under my bed.

The yard is fenced so my pastime is hidden from the road. I throw a knife – it lands directly in the bark – less gouge at the center of the trunk from where I stand. I've been doing this for a while. Some people do puzzles. I realize I'm not your average girl. I never went for fuzzy, frilly, sparkly and pink; I was always more of a... well, *this*. I'm not saying I don't like girly things — I do — I like jewelry and stuff. You will never see me wear a piece of jewelry for more than two hours though. I physically *cannot* do it. I *have* to take it off. Yes, my commitment issues are *that* bad. And when I say I can't do it, I mean I *literally can't*. I become claustrophobic. I can wear earrings, but that's about it. I got the ones I'm wearing three months ago and I haven't taken them off since I bought them and put them in. Maybe it's because the hoops are small and I completely forget about them.

I throw another knife and watch it land to the side, slightly lower than the first one. The last one lands the wrong way, handle stuck into the wood. Ugh. That's going to bug me. I walk over and pull the knives out of the tree starting with the backwards one.

I learned from my mother how important appearance is, so I guess I owe it to her that I started working out. I wouldn't have the toned body I do if I didn't start off life as self-conscious as I did. I learned a lot growing up with her, though there were some lessons she probably didn't intend to teach me. Such as the unspoken lesson of *don't give a fuck, because you're not going to please everyone, or even anyone for that matter.* Which brings me to number two, self-confidence and self-reliance. I learned how to build up my self-confidence by working out, because hey, if you look good, you feel good, and you have no physical reason to feel self-conscious. What do you have to worry about, right? Whole bunch of birds, one stone. I got really good at finding things I'm good at, like flipping butterfly knives, for starters.

Dad gave me my first butterfly knife when I was nine years old. God, I loved that thing – sliced my fingers up pretty good when first started flipping it, but that didn't stop me. I played with it so much it started falling apart whenever I opened it. So the next one he got me didn't come from an army surplus store, it came from some renowned cutlery website, and it was gorgeous. From then on, I was hooked. Butterfly knives, karambits, throwing knives... it's all that was ever on my birthday and Christmas lists. And I know how to use them. It kind of freaked Mom out just because I was a girl and it wasn't all dolls, miniskirts and baking. But don't worry, she made sure I knew I was depriving her of the joys of having a daughter. My dad on the other hand, was thrilled. No one was ever going to mess with me.

As cynical as I sound it really doesn't bother me anymore... hasn't in a long time.

4.

Smarts

I arrive at the place on the street at where I can see my house after finishing my run. Immediately my eyes set on a very large, very black vehicle in the driveway, which effectively stops me in my tracks. No wonder drug dealers have tinted windows – they're quite intimidating. Maybe it's *not* a serial killer, maybe it's just someone who's lost... parked to look at a map... in my driveway... when he or she could have even more easily pulled over to the side of the road. Maybe they were hoping to ring my doorbell and ask for directions. Or to use the bathroom, or the phone, or something... which would be very strange and I would have definitely denied their request. Maybe it's that guy Frida was talking about and polluting my phone with pictures of... Yeah, it might be him... driving around in a sketchy ass rape-van. I can see her giving out information like my home address. But he wouldn't just show up on my doorstep... Would he? Well, whoever it is, at least my car's at the shop so there's no evidence that anyone is home.

Turning around, I walk back down the hill. Seems logical. This doesn't make me a chicken, it makes me a person with a proper working brain. See Max, I'm no dunce. Sketchy ass rape-van equals get the fuck out of there. I'd rather avoid confrontation with whoever that was. I have a bad feeling, and I typically run on instinct. I walk into the turn that brings me back into the circle then take off into a run. I probably should be doing another lap anyway.

After I finish a couple more laps, I figure I should probably call Frida and see if she gave that guy my address. I slow to a walk and catch my breath for a few strides before I pull out my cell phone and click on her contact in my favorites.

She picks up on the second ring.

"Hello?"

Her greeting is slightly slurred. Jesus! It's like noon!

"Hey" I chuckle. "You alright there?"

"Yeah, yeah, what's up?" She giggles back and clears her throat, unsuccessfully trying to compose herself.

"Hey, I just wanted to know if you gave that Michael guy my address?"

"What? Oh! No, I did not." She finishes enthusiastically with a big laugh.

She isn't being facetious, she's just wasted.

"Why? Do you want his number?" She continues with heavy enthusiasm.

"No thanks, I'm good. Who's with you?"

"Roommate and her boyfriend. It's cool." She's assures me.

"Alright, stay safe. 'Kay?"

"M 'kay" The smile evident in her voice.

"'Kay, I'll talk to you later"

"'Kay, talk to you later, bye."

She's gone and the music comes back on through my headphones. I really miss Frida, she's more sister than best friend. After two years of attending community college here, she convinced her parents to fund her dream of attending art school in New York. Growing up, it was always her, my brother and me – the three amigos. Now I'm the last amigo left here, with Bruce off in Florida and then moving into his college dorm when he gets back, and Frida all the way in New York, I've gone up there for a weekend already and she's only been living there for a month. She was so concerned about me not having anyone to hang out with when she left. I mean, this is Rhode Island. New York is only about four hours away... but that's *far enough* to be far away.'

I speed up and finish the circle, making my way back up the street to my house for a second time. The truck is not in my driveway. I take a couple more steps and clear the fence to find out that it hasn't gone far. It's up the road a little straddling the curb. I'll take it. I make my way to the front door and let myself in. Pulling out my ear buds, I head for the bathroom, tossing my phone on the counter to wait for my return.

After emptying my bladder and throwing on a clean tank top and pair of jeans, I return to the kitchen and disconnect my phone from the headphones, sticking it into my back pocket and leaving the twisted cord on the counter. I check the stew then begin to rummage through the cupboards for a box of macaroni and cheese.

BANG!

The smash rips my attention away from my search for food. What the hell?

BANG!

The front door caves in and four men dressed all in black decked out in bulletproof vests and tactical gear pour into the house.

"Secure the package!" One man shouts.

All four men have a silenced handgun trained on me so I put my hands where they can be seen.

"What the fuck?" I utter in shock.

"We need her in that truck in three," the same man spouts authoritatively.

"What?" I demand though my bewilderment. "What the hell is going on?"

"Cuff her!"

"What? No! You're not gonna cuff me! Somebody tell me what the fuck is going on!"

They make their way over to me. Two of them grab my arms, force them behind my back, and push me down onto the counter. Another slaps metal handcuffs on my wrists.

"Hey! What the hell! You can't do this! I haven't done anything!"

They pull me back up and start walking me to the front door.

"Hey! Someone fucking talk to me! What do you think I did? Hey!"

I strain against their pull, trying to yank my arms away from them, but it's as if I'm not fighting back at all. I slump and try to fall to the floor but they lift me up and continue to drag me along toward the open door. I was hoping that would slow them down a little, but no. I start flailing again and pushing back with my feet to try to stop them from getting me to the door. I look to the guy on my right.

"Hey! You can't do this! What do you think I did?"

He continues to ignore me and my efforts, I just want to slap his face.

"Hey!" I shout at him directly.

Then we stop somewhat abruptly but he still doesn't look at me, so I know my voice is not what caused this halt. What's he staring at? I lean forward to see. There in the door stands by far the most attractive young man I've ever seen. He shifts his narrowed ice-blue eyes back and forth between the two men that are holding me in place. His short dirty blond hair is delicately tossed around in the mild breeze. His cocky crooked smile fails to touch those gorgeous eyes or his furrowed brows. Then his eyes narrow further, making his smirk match even less.

"How's it going, boys?"

His words ooze a certain sarcasm. Like he's trying, but not really, to make it seem like he's just here to chat. This guy is pissed! At me?

As he continues to glare, the grips on my arms tighten. These men are afraid of him. Who is he? He can't be much older than I am, how could he possibly have a reputation that would frighten these, clearly trained, professionals.

My eyes trail down from his facial region and up his toned arm to the gun he has fixed on my forehead. Do these men work for him? Is that why they're afraid of him? Were they bringing me to him? Maybe I *was* slowing them down and they were taking too long to get me outside, so he came to see what the holdup was. I've never seen this guy before in my life! Why would he want me dead?

Maybe this is all a mistake. I'm getting pretty fucking pissed now. Outraged, I tear my eyes from the sight of the handgun in my face and return my renewed glare to his eyes. The subtle movement causes him to notice me for the first time and the smug crooked smile that's been on his face, is interrupted. His lips slowly cover his teeth as his jaw drops ever so slightly. His eyes soften as he tilts his head. I continue to stare as he evidently tries to firm up again, gritting his teeth as if frustrated.

His gun takes a significant turn and fires at the man on my right. I turn to see the man's head bob back. He crumples to the floor. Oh my god! He's dead! In my house! This guy was just shot down in cold blood *at my front door*!

The man behind me pulls me back and pushes me to the floor. I make an effort to land mostly on my right shoulder, holding my face up.

No one is holding onto me, so I flip over into a sitting position. All three of the remaining agents are being occupied by Mr. Angry Eyes. I push myself away from the fray with my feet and dart my eyes to the body of the dead man on the floor not too far from where I sit. He must have a key on him, right? Only way to find out... Oh I really don't want to do this! I roll back over onto my knees and stand up, then dive backward to the dead guy's side. I look over my shoulder at his belt loops, hoping… Yes! Keys! A whole ring… fuck. I reach and grab it, yank once, twice, then a third time using all my weight flinging my whole body forward. The loop finally gives and I fall forward. With the keys in my hand, I roll to my knees and stand again. I run for the kitchen to get behind a counter. I turn to catch a glimpse of the jumbled mess by the front door. *Angry Eyes* is twisting the arm of one of the now two remaining men and knocking him to the floor. The gun he's holding goes off while facing me, the bullet grazes my left bicep.

I let out a quick "Ah!" and spin on my heel, falling to the floor. I drop the keys in the fall so I roll back onto them to pick them up. I look back to see that the quarrel has frozen and all faces are turned to me. Shit! I look away and scramble back to my feet, heading for the cover of kitchen counter again. The shouts of agony at the front door resume as I arrive at my destination. Leaning against the drawers, I begin going through the keys on the ring. There are only two different sets of feet shuffling around now. Come on! Come on! I fiddle quickly, trying to get each key to turn. Finally, one works. I get the cuff off my left hand and pull my hands in front of me to remove the other, but the clatter of the brawl stops. I freeze.

5.

Upside Down

The sound of footsteps approaches the kitchen. My heart is a deafening sound, thundering through my head. I look up at the wall above the counter at the magnetic strip that holds our good knife set. I drop the handcuff key to the floor and jump up, grab a knife, turn it in my hand so the blade is facing down, then turn to face whoever is responsible for the approaching footsteps in a defensive stance, letting the open cuff dangle off my right wrist. The culprit is Angry Eyes, whose eyes have since mellowed out.

"Whoa, whoa, whoa! Easy killer," he laughs weakly, holding his hands up at the level of his face. A defensive stance?

Or is it just to show me his hands? To show me he's not holding the gun? So now he doesn't want to shoot me?

"What the fuck is going on?" I demand, although it comes out as somewhat of a shriek.

"Sorry about your arm. That was my bad..."

I look down at my arm. Blood has trailed all the way to my hand and is now dripping to the floor off my elbow. When I look back up at the man he is closer to me, but he isn't currently moving.

"So, you're Sophie Fileux, right?"

"Who wants to know?"

"I'll take that as a yes," he smiles.

"Glad to know you were gonna shoot me before you were sure."

"Sophie, if I was *gonna* shoot you I'd 'a done it by now, so you can relax and put the knife away"

"No thank you."

"Alright now I realize you're probably under a lot stress —"

"Stress?" I screech.

"But I need you to pull it together, OK?"

"Pull it together? Oh I'm fine, I'm fine, I'm together. I just got fucking shot! OK? Start talking! Who are you?"

"Kael."

I hold my stance and wait for him to continue talking.

"You wanna put that knife down now?"

"Not really, no. You wanna tell me what's going on?" I blurt impatiently.

"Not even a little, Sophie, but I *am* going to need you to come with me, so…" he claps his hands lightly twice and sends his thumbs gesturing over his right shoulder toward the front door.

"I'm not going anywhere with you! You just killed those guys! And like five seconds ago you were going to kill me!"

"Look," He sighs. "For arguments sake, let's agree that you're in over your head *with the pending situation.* You are coming with me because *you need me.* You are not equipped to handle what's coming at you." He cocks his head to one side, looking at me like this is common sense that I should know.

"My dad's a cop. I don't need any help from you."

"This really isn't up for debate," he sighs, turning to check the front door.

"You're right, actually, it's not up for debate. So why are you still here?"

He sniffs as a grin spreads across his face. He looks up at the ceiling briefly and places his hands on his hips before returning his over-confident gaze to me.

"I'm giving you a choice of leaving this house in one of two ways. OK? One way being with dignity. The other way is going to land you in the trunk. So what's it gonna be?"

"Try me!" I growl, narrowing my eyes at him. I raise the knife higher. "I dare you!"

Exasperation takes a toll on his grin.

"Those guys," he points at the pile of dead bodies, "there's gonna be more of them. Probably very soon. I need you to work with me here. We really need to leave. Like. Now."

"What do they want?"

"I think you already know the answer to that. Which brings us back to the fact that you need to let me help you."

"That's not what I mean! I mean why? And what does this have to do with you? Why should I trust you? Why would you *help* me?"

"Good question. I'll let you know when I figure that out."

Suddenly his attention is dramatically yanked to something behind me. The window? Are there more armed men ready to come in through the back? Panicked, I turn to see what he's looking at. There's nothing unusual that *I* can see.

In an instant, the knife is out of my hand and thrown onto the counter and I find myself thrown over the shoulder of this mysterious stranger.

"Hey!"

"This is for your own good, Soph. Trust me."

"No! Let go of me!"

His arm is wrapped tightly over my thighs, just above my knees, so I can't swing my calf up high enough to kick him in the face.

"Put me down! I mean it!"

"I mean it too. You need my help."

I ball my hands into fists and begin beating on his back, twisting to try and throw off his center of gravity. He ignores my efforts, is completely unaffected, and makes his way to the front door. When the wall comes within reach, I grabbed at the first thing I have access to… a mirror! Perfect. I pull it down and swing it over my back, effectively smashing it over his head.

"AGH!"

He takes a sharp gasp of air, sucking it in through his clenched teeth. I use the opportunity to roll dramatically outward, effectively releasing myself and falling to the floor. Landing on my back knocks the wind out of me but the adrenaline rush I gave myself with the mirror trick allows me to disregard that. I roll over and quickly scan the floor for the right shaped shard of broken mirror to use as a weapon. Singling one out, I pick it up and turn it over, pointy end down. I jump to my feet and send a right hook in front of his face, skimming his left cheekbone with the sharp tip of mirrored glass.

"AH!"

Swiftly touching the tips of his fingers to the new slice under his eye and pulling them away to look at the blood, he throws his hands up in a fighting stance to guard his face.

"That all you got?" He asks.

He isn't so much challenging me, as he's humoring me. It's clear in his voice and all over his playful expression. It's really pissing me off. He doesn't think I can take him. Ass-fucking-hole. As usual, I'm ready to correct such assumptions. I bring my right foot up to roundhouse kick him in the head but he catches my foot and holds onto it, using it to shove me back into the wall behind me before letting it go. I drop the shard of glass as I catch and steady myself against the wall. I look up at him, and he's just standing there watching, waiting for me to throw something else at him.

"You done?"

Fuming, I fling myself at him once more, swinging my arms in a series of punches and elbow jabs, missing every time as he ducks, dodges, and pushes my arm out of its path. Finally, I land my fist on his right eye. His head bounces away from the impact. I give him no time to recover, launching into a back kick that he catches and uses to knock me off my balance. I stumble back, falling into the wall again. Quickly, I push myself up and resume my fighting stance.

"I don't need your help!"

"Are you fucking kidding me?" He laughs. "Were you not here like five minutes ago? What would you have done if I was not here to save your ass?"

"Why should I believe you're here to help me? Maybe it was *you* who wasn't here five minutes ago. You had a gun pointed at my head!"

"No, see, I was *definitely* here five minutes ago. It's actually why *you're* still here."

"Ooo, clever."

"No. Fact. And that's a problem for me. Now, there will be more of those men coming to get you. I don't see any options for you other than to come with me. So what's the bottleneck here? From your point of view — please enlighten me."

A problem for him?

"Enlighten you?"

"Yes."

"Enlighten me! I don't know what the fuck's going on!"

"The time it's gonna take me to make you understand is a lot longer than what we have time for right now."

The wind-chopping sound of helicopter blades is suddenly apparent and growing in volume.

"Shit." Kael breathes.

"Is that them?"

Shit! Shit! Shit! I'm immediately anxious. I don't want to go with them! I don't particularly want to go with him either, but...

"What do we do?" I inquire apprehensively.

"Oh thank god," he sighs appreciatively. "What a relief! I thought I was gonna have to knock you out."

He smirks.

"Would you stop? Please. Just... tell me what to do."

After a moment more of flashing his bright white teeth, he strikes a more serious expression.

"Back door. We head for the woods; they won't be able to see us through the trees. That's how we disappear. Now move. We have to run. Keep up with me."

He starts to sprint through the kitchen to the slider but doesn't turn his eyes from me until I'm mirroring his actions.

"Ready for this?" he asks, resting his hand on the door handle.

I can barely hear him over this new pounding in my head.

"Yeah."

6.

Gun Tricks

He yanks the door open and takes off across the deck to the grass. I follow. He's fast but I keep up. When we're halfway across the yard, he turns, pulling his pistol out of his pants at the small of his back. I watch in amazement as the gun twirls gracefully in his hand into a firing position. He's pointing up at the sky. He fires two shots. I turn to see a limp parashooter floating toward the Earth, head drooped to one side. Dead.

"Don't worry about it! Just get to the damn trees!" He scolds.

I turn around and run toward him. He fires another two shots as I pass by. I make it past the first few trees and turn to check and see where he is.

"Go, Go, Go!" He shouts.

He's running toward me. The helicopter is landing in the yard behind him. I turn and run more, losing my footing in some tree roots. He's at my side in seconds already standing me back up before I even hit the ground. As he let's go and leads me further into the woods I sneak a quick glance at the helicopter to see two more heavily armed men leap out. Catching up to him quickly, we weave through the trees as fast as our legs can take us. Once we've put enough distance between us and the men, he comes to a quick halt. I stop, catching myself so that I don't crash into him.

"Why'd we stop? What are we doing?" I ask frantically.

"Which direction will bring us to the closest house?"

I point slightly to the right of the path we've already been running on.

The rustling of feet is no longer in the distance.

"Come on." He orders with quiet urgency.

We take off in the direction I pointed.

"THERE!" I hear from behind me.

Kael whips around and raises his gun.

I start to turn and see who he's about to shoot, but I'm halted by an alarming pinch in my neck. I hear the distinct sound of Kael's silenced handgun go off. And then the rustle of leaves as the body crashes to the forest floor. Touching my neck, I quickly find the answer to the mystery of the pinch. It feels like a dart. Kael's gun goes off a couple more times. I wrap my fingers around the dart and pluck it out. Examining it slightly dazed, I conclude that it looks like a shot, like what you would see at doctor's office, only a quarter of the size.

"Shit," Kael utters.

I rip my gaze from the dart and look at him. He's much closer than I remember him being.

"What is it?" I slur.

Why am I slurring?

"Let me see."

I take a step toward him, quickly noticing my leg feels extremely heavy... and numb.

He takes it from my hand and examines it.

"Here, Com'ere, I gotcha," he sighs, chucking the dart over his shoulder.

He snakes his arm under both of mine.

"I feel really weird..." It took a lot longer to get that sentence out than it should have.

"Yeah, you're gonna pass out in few seconds."

He dips his shoulder down to one side and scoops up my legs.

"You alright?" He asks starting to jog forward.

"No... I..."

"You're alright, Soph." He chuckles. "You're alright."

The world has begun to blur and grow darker and darker…

7.

Socks

A gentle rocking soothes me into consciousness. My eyes flutter open and then close back up, too comfortable to look at the world yet. I love car rides. So calming... Sometimes I like to go on road trips just for the drive. I hate it when it ends... wait, what? Car? How? My eyes open to see the unfamiliar back of an unfamiliar passenger seat. I'm curled up in the back of an unfamiliar car. Where am I now? How far have we traveled? How long could I have been out for? It was drug induced so... I have no idea.

"Where'd this car come from?

"Jesus!" He flinches, flying forward against his seat belt. "It was so quiet... Jeez." He takes a breath, composes himself before continuing. "Hotwired it."

"Of course you did. You know, you're making it very difficult for me to trust you."

He chuckles.

"How long have I been out?"

"Couple hours."

"Where are we?"

"Massachusetts."

I sit up and look out the window. Trees... not very telling. I go to scratch my arm to satisfy an itch but my finger meets a rough fabric instead of skin. He bandaged my arm... with... what is this?

"Is this a sock?"

"It's all I had to work with." He turns to look at me in the back seat with that signature cocky smirk of his. "Maybe if you had been friendlier, I might have put more effort into finding you a suitable bandage. Keep that in mind for next time."

I narrow my eyes.

"Your feet reek by the way. Good job."

I climb over the center console into the front, sit myself in the passenger seat and buckle my seat belt.

"So where are we going?"

"Boston"

"Why"

"I live there."

"Isn't that a place they would come looking for us. They obviously know who you are."

"They don't know *this* place. I just need to pick up some stuff."

I sit for a moment and stare out the window. We're passing small shopping plazas now. I open the window and partially stick my head out. I still feel a bit groggy. What was that sedative?

"How did you clean all the blood, by the way?" I ask, inspecting the knuckles I partially busted up when I punched him in the face.

"Fast food joint. Drive-thru. Got a big cup a water and a bunch 'a napkins… speaking of food, you hungry?"

I look up at him from my hand.

He lifts a greasy looking bag up from beneath his seat and holds it out for me.

"I went through 'bout half hour back, shouldn't be too cold. Got you a burger… left you some fries too, but they're probably nasty by now."

Great, just what I need. Diarrhea.

"I'm not eating that."

"Why not?"

"I don't eat cow, and I don't eat fast food."

"Oh, God."

"Food is food. Just eat it."

"That is a bullshit statement, and I'm *not* going to eat it."

"Take the burger!"

I grab the bag from his hand and toss it out my window.

"What the hell?" He shouts.

"Tell me what's going on. Now."

He sighs, exasperated.

"You'd have a hard time believing me."

"How convenient for you."

"I'm serious. Can't you just trust me on this? I'm obviously on your side."

"On my side of *what*? If you want me to trust you, you're gonna have to give me some answers. You could be some crazy psycho who's escaped from an insane asylum"

"If I were, I'd probably lie."

That's true.

"That makes me feel better. You're *good* at this."

"Come on, Soph. Knowing is not going to make this *any* easier for you. Your life as you know it is gone anyway. Humor me; what've you got to lose?"

"No. Now. You implied earlier that you would tell me if I came with you. Well here I am."

"When did I *imply* that?" He snickers.

"You said there wasn't enough time earlier."

"That's not implying anything."

He tries but fails to mask a smirk.

"Ugh! This isn't fair! Why is this happening to me?"

I look away and slam my back against my seat.

He stops smiling and I see him look at me in my peripheral vision, but I keep my eyes on the road ahead.

"I know it isn't, and I'm sorry you're a part of this... if I could make you off limits I would, but I can't."

For a moment I don't know what to say. I wish he would just tell me what's going on. Maybe if I just ask the right question, I can at least satisfy myself for now.

"You were going to kill me."

"At the time... in my plan... making you *off limits* did not require that you stay alive."

"Ah. Yes. That makes sense now." I grumble under my breath.

"I was mad." His interruption has a new tone that makes me turn my head to face him.

He's the one with his eyes glued to the road now. I wait for him to continue. He might finally be giving something away.

"The last one they took was my friend. I have to make sure they don't get what they're after. They don't get to *take* whatever they want. They don't get to. I won't let them. I grew up with him, he was..."

He stops talking and smacks the steering wheel with his palm, making me jump slightly in my seat.

"He was my responsibility... my *only* responsibility... and I..."

I stare at him, once again, without any words to say.

"Why did they take him?"

Maybe I can determine why *I'm* the target now if I know why they took *him*. He looks at me, his expression unreadable despite his furrowed brows. Maybe he's searching for words himself? Maybe he's just looking for the right words to answer my question, yet keep me in the dark? The thought frustrates me, but I don't let it touch my face. He hasn't actually said anything yet. Maybe I should give him the benefit of the doubt.

"For the same reason they're after you now."

Fuck you, benefit of the doubt! I have to keep him talking, maybe he'll slip.

"So what changed?"

"What?"

"You were going to shoot me out of revenge for your friend. I'm still here, why?" I shrug.

He looks at me again, gauging my expression.

"I don't know. I looked at you... and I couldn't do it. Which, believe me, is big deal for me. Killing people is what I do for a living."

I shoot my gaze at him again. His eyes are back on the road, but he turns his head slightly to meet mine for a moment, when he realizes I'm staring at him.

"And why is that, exactly?"

"I'm an assassin. Or a hitter, as we call it"

Holy shit! Then again that was a pretty impressive display earlier at the house. So not exactly surprising.

"Hitter?"

"Hitter." He nods his head.

"Have you ever been shot?"

I honestly don't know why that's the first question that popped out of my mouth.

"Many times."

"Then you must not be very good," I quip.

I smile inwardly, very proud of myself.

"Because *everyone's* reaction upon meeting a trained killer is to *piss them off*. You are truly something else."

He can't hide his amusement.

"But at least you're resourceful," I add, pointing at the sock tied on my arm.

"Hey!" He stops to laugh. "I've been in the game for a long time. A lot of time to acquire some injuries. And I wouldn't talk after you went and got yourself shot." He pokes my bandaged arm.

The pressure causes a sharp stab of pain.

"Ah! Hey!" I grab my dressed wound.

He laughs as I glare at him.

"Where we're going, we can get you some stitches for that if it needs any."

I ignore his amusement and reattach my gaze to the road.

"How long? I mean how old are you? You can't be much older than me."

"I'm two years older than you."

"How do you know? I never told you how old I am."

"You were born in 1991."

"I thought you said you didn't *know* who I am?"

"I knew *of* you." He states matter-of-factly.

"*Of* me? What else is there to know *of* me? Why is everyone all the sudden so interested in me? Cause I know this isn't because of something I did. I didn't *do* anything!"

He's silent.

"Did I?"

"No, you didn't do anything wrong, Soph." He sounds sympathetic. "I know this isn't fair. It's not. You don't deserve this."

His angel face looks so sad; I realize I've become accustomed to his cocky grin. Sadness looks alien on him. I need to change the subject.

"I'm hungry," I blurt

"Oh I'm sorry, you pitched your rations out the window. Remember?"

"I haven't eaten in hours. I need food. We're on the same side, right? Well, take me to an organic food store."

"Oh my God. You're one of *those*."

"What's *that* supposed to mean?"

"Ugh, nothing."

"What?" I demand.

"*Nothing*."

8.

Lighters

We pull into a space in the grocery store parking lot, and Kael turns off the car and looks at me.

"What do you want?"

"I'm going in, too."

"I don't think so."

"*Try* and stop me." I challenge, narrowing my eyes at him.

I turn, grab the door handle, and start to push open the door, but he reaches past me and pulls it closed. Then in the same movement and with the same hand, he grabs the empty cuff dangling from my wrist and slaps it onto the door grip.

"Hey!"

"Incidentally, you have a handcuff on your wrist, which could attract attention that we don't want. Not to mention a bloody sock tied to your arm. So sit tight, and I'll go grab some energy bars. Any preferences?"

"I can't believe you just did that! What if those guys come? You can't leave me stuck here! And you have a cut under your eye!"

He had cleaned it up, so it doesn't look really look all that bad but I don't have anything else to use against him.

"I'll get you something chocolate flavored then," he smirks." I won't be long."

I slam my back into the seat and stare forward. Out of the corner of my eye I see his oh-so-proud-of-himself smile expand, and he's through the door shutting it quickly behind him. With one more look at me through the window he sprints off to the store entrance.

Immediately I start rummaging through the glove box for something, anything, I can try picking the lock on this cuff with. Nothing. Not a safety pin, not a bobby pin, nothing. Just the vehicle's registration, manual, and bunch of junk papers. Not that I know a bobby pin or safety pin would have worked. All there is in the center console are a couple of burned disks and a lighter. Hmm... I pick up the lighter and flick it on. Butane. Nice. Maybe... I let go of the trigger and position it below the door grip.

Maybe I could melt through this. It's a long shot but I don't have any short shots available, so what the hell. I flick it on again and hold it steady.

It starts to melt the top coating anyway. He has really pretty eyes... Kael... the rest of him is pretty enjoyable to look at as well... why am I thinking about this? Maybe it's because this is the first guy I've ever been *really* attracted to. Finally I know for sure that its possible. I was beginning to think I was asexual. Thank God... it turns out I'm just shallow... *No! Stop it! You can't be attracted to him! He's dangerous! He just told you that he's an assassin. What's wrong with you?* But... I'm not afraid of him. I never was. How can that be?

I'm finally beginning to make a real dent in the door grip. There's no way there's enough fluid in this lighter to last *that* much longer...

The driver's side door swings open, startling me.

"You having fun over there?" Kael asks.

I let the button go.

"Oh yeah, just passing the time, you know."

He stares at me in what looks like amazement. My resourcefulness? Or is he catching on to the fact that I will always have something to say at times like these?

"Cute," he decides on.

"Not my intention," I assure him.

"Give it to me."

I absorb the lighter into a tight fist. He holds up the grocery bag for me to see.

"You want your food? You give me that." He finishes pointing at my hand.

Ugh! I toss the lighter at his chest, but his reflexes allow him to secure it there. He pinches it between his fingers and puts it into his front right pocket before giving me the bag.

"Great, now it smells like burning plastic in here." He complains.

I reach in and pull out one of the energy bars.

"Well you're the one who handcuffed me to a car door. This is what happens."

I rip open the wrapper and take a bite.

"I want this off, *now*, by the way." I say, not caring to finish swallowing my bite first.

"I can't get it off *this second*, I don't have a key."

I stop chewing and dart my eyes up at his face.

"You don't have the key?" I say with my mouth still full. "I thought you must have grabbed it when you threw me over your shoulder! Why else would you do *this* if you didn't have the key?" I stop talking to swallow, "I can't deal with this! I can't! I need it off! Get it off! You don't understand, I need this off, right now!"

"*We'll stop* at a hardware store; I'll grab something to get it off. Keep your panties on." He chuckles.

"Oh they're *staying* on!"

Why did I say that? He looks at me, a smile spreading uninhibited on his face, but he doesn't say anything. I turn and resort to staring out the passenger window on the side of me. Frustration overtakes me as I flail my bonded wrist in a small scale, short-lived tantrum.

"Calm down, I'll have it off soon." He assures.

I say nothing, and just continue to stare out the window, doing my best to pretend he's not there.

9.

Corners

He's been in there for a while now. He parked us in a secluded part of the lot, way in the back of the side of the store against the wall. Does he even know how to pick a lock? Maybe he doesn't know what he needs. I grab my phone out of my back pocket. Maybe I can find out how on the Internet. I type in the search bar 'how to pick a lock,' click on the first video on the list, and begin to watch the intro in which the host is introducing himself.

A knock on my window makes me jump. I look up at a man who is staring in and looking at the cuff on my wrist. Shit! I wave shyly at him with my free arm. He circles his finger, signaling me to roll down the window. Shit! Lucky Kael left the keys in the ignition so I could leave the air conditioning on. It makes the situation look better. If I were being held against my will, the kidnapper wouldn't leave me with the car keys.

I pause the video, rest the phone on the armrest beside me and press the window button on the door.

"Hi" I greet the man awkwardly.

"Are you alright?" He asks, the concern in his voice, very evident.

"Yeah, yeah, I'm fine. I just..."

Shit! what do I say?

"Do you need help? I can get someone for you."

"No, no! I'm fine! Really!"

Another man walks up and joins the man outside the car. I have no idea where he came from.

"Is everything alright?"

Oh God help me! This figures... who knew there were good fucking Samaritans in the world.

"Miss, why don't you open the door." The first man instructs, trying for a soothing tone.

Maybe he thinks I'm in denial.

"No, it's OK I really don't −"

The second man reaches in the window and unlocks the door then grabs the outside handle and pulls.

"I was just messing around with these handcuffs and got myself stuck."

Messing around with handcuffs and they just happened to end up like this? Stupid. Maybe I should say that I'm practicing a magic act. No. Also dumb.

The second man proceeds to yank the door, pulling me along with it. I am pulled from the car, having just enough time to position my feet so I can land in a standing position outside the vehicle.

"Hey, easy!" I shout.

Suddenly I feel uncomfortable after the man's abrasiveness.

"What the hell?" I add.

"Settle down." The first man says in a hushed tone lifting his shirt so I can see the gun tucked into the front of his pants.

Fuck! Not good Samaritans! Not good Samaritans!

The second man grabs hold of my bicep opposite the handcuff.

"Get your hand *off* me!"

I whip myself out of his grasp but the second I do, he grabs me again tighter, at my elbow this time, and pushes me into the inside of the door, effectively pinning my bonded arm behind my back. My eyes are immediately drawn to the shimmer of light that reflects off his knife as he pulls it out of his pants and raises it up to rest it on my waist so I can feel it's sharp edge. I look up at his face, and he's smiling.

"It would be a shame to *waste* a pretty girl like you," he starts darkly.

He presses the metal tip lightly but promisingly into my lower abdomen and twists ever so slightly. "Who did you come here with?"

"He doesn't have the key," I snap, clenching my fist and struggling against his hold.

"That's not what I asked you." He leans into me, pressing harder with the knife. It's broken the skin now. I feel the knife slowly slicing into me. The feeling is sickening. I think this is the worse pain I have ever felt in my life. Worse than the gun shot earlier.

I take in a sharp intake of breath through my nose but hold back all the noises that threaten to surface. I refuse to give him any satisfaction.

"I can make this a lot more painful. Now, I want to know who they sent to pick you up."

I say nothing, glaring at him. This seems to be all I'm good for today.

Slowly the knife burrows deeper into my abdomen.

"I'm going to ask you again. Who..." Deeper. "Is..." Twisting "It...?"

"Aha!" I gasp and suck air through my teeth.

His mouth drops open a little but the corners curl up as he narrows his eyes.

I feel sick to my stomach. But I continue to glare all the same.

"Ay!" Kael's voice rings into my ears.

I've never been so happy to hear someone's voice in my *life*. I look in the direction. He's closing in with an ax slung over his shoulder.

"What do you say we settle this like... you know what? I'm not sure I know how to be a gentleman." He finishes with a smirk, rocking the ax on his shoulder. "I *do* know how to be an *honest* man though, that's why I can *honestly* tell you that this is *not* going to end well for you guys." He lifts the ax, readying it like he's waiting for a pitch. "But don't worry. I'll make it look like an *ax*-ident."

The first man whips the gun out of his pants. In one swing, Kael removes the gun and the hand of Number One. Before he even gets to process what's happened, Kael spins and plants a back kick on side of his head. Number Two lets go of my arm, and the knife is removed from my flesh. I gasp with relief. The knife is then slashed at Kael's throat, ducking, Kael allows it to finish in its current path before reaching up and grabbing the arm holding it. He's practically a blur as he twists and turns sending Number Two over his shoulder. The second he's on the ground, the ax follows catching him in the chest.

"Holy shit!" I utter and cover my mouth with my free hand.

Blood squirts everywhere. Number One is screaming on the ground now. Kael picks up the gun with Number One's hand still attached, separates the two, and shoots him in the head.

I stare at the bloody mess in front of me. This guy really knows how to... do this.

"Lift your shirt."

His words snap me out of my daze and I look up at him.

"Excuse me?"

"Your shirt, lift it. You're bleeding, show me the wound."

"I'm fine."

"Sophie, how deep did he get you? I need to see."

I look down and see all the red soaking my shirt. Maybe I'm *not* fine. He is *apparently* the expert on this stuff. I drag the sticky wet material up over my abdomen, stopping in the middle of my ribcage. Immediately he bends down on one knee to in spect, placing a warm hand on my stomach beside the bloody hole. I flinch a little. He looks up at me, concerned.

"Tickles."

He tries but fails to hide a smile as he looks back at my exposed skin.

"You work out," he says matter of factly.

"Are you checking to see if I'll live or did you just want to see my muscle definition?"

"Both."

I swat his hand away, push my shirt back down and shoot my knee up, knocking him in the nose.

"Ah, shit!" His head flies back and he covers his nose. "Yeah, I deserved that. Your cut is fine, it's not too deep. We gotta get it cleaned up though, make sure it doesn't get infected."

"This is *your* fault!"

He lowers his hand and his gaze sags to the ground.

"I know."

He's... regretful? I wasn't expecting that. I thought he'd deny it and say something annoyingly witty. I'm caught off guard, but I'm still not satisfied.

"Why did you *stick* me here!" I shout, tugging vigorously against my bond.

"I'm sorry." He continues.

"This wouldn't have happened if you didn't – ugh! What the fuck took you so long in there? Did you even get anything to pick this with?" I look him over. No plastic bags.

"I'm sorry!" He repeats desperately, standing up and grabbing my shoulders. "I'm sorry I left you alone! I'm sorry I left you defenseless like that! I'm sorry I let you get hurt! It'll never happen again, I promise. I've never had to worry about anyone else besides me before–" he pauses, seemingly remembering something. Like his confession applies to something else as well. "I... I'm sorry."

The change in him makes me almost sorry for yelling at him. I just stare back at him for a moment, his proximity starting to affect my stomach. Butterflies? Is that what this is? I look away so he can't see my eyes because I feel my cheeks getting warm, and I don't want him to see me blush.

"You really made a mess." I shift the subject some, refocusing my gaze on the dead, mostly to distract myself. "Is this a professional job here? 'Cause I thought you guys were supposed to make clean kills."

"No, that right there," he gestures with his work with eyes. "Is a resourceful kill."

He smirks. Also seeming relieved by the conversation's new direction. He gazes fondly at the ax.

"Axes are fun," he adds, releasing my shoulders.

I raise my eyebrows at him in disbelief.

"You're a psycho." I shake my head and roll my eyes away.

What am I doing? This guy is insane. I should not be relieved by his presence.

"What happened to *your* gun?" I ask.

"Out of bullets. I'll take this one with me," he pats the gun he apparently stuck in his pocket after pulling a hand off it. "We'll stock up on bullets and supplies when we stop at my place."

Leaning over, he grabs hold of the ax and yanks hard, removing it from its resting spot and wipes it on a clean spot of the dead guy's pants.

"I came up with a plan — move," he instructs, swatting the air.

I step to the side understanding what he plans to do.

"Did you?" I prompt.

"We're going to Nebraska." He raises the ax and swings it down on the door grip beside the cuff. I know he's not aiming for my hand, but the motion makes me jump anyway.

"Oh?" I prod again.

"I got someone there who can help. He's there on a job right now."

"Kind of a long drive."

"Eh, couple days. It'll be fun."

The second chop provides a space wide enough to fit the cuff through. I slide the metal through the opening. Now I'm disconnected from the door, but not the cuffs themselves. An improvement for sure, but...

"OK, now how do we get *this* off?" I ask shaking my cuff-occupied wrist.

"Would you relax? Come on." He gestures his head toward the heavily occupied area of the parking lot. "We need to get out of here first. Someone must have seen us by now; cops are probably on their way."

"But… UGH!" I shake my wrist again.

"You have my word. I am not going to cuff you to anything else. OK? Now let's go."

He starts walking. I caress my abdomen and follow. This does not feel good… it's kind of a zinging pain. The skin seems to separate with every step I take. Wait, my phone!

"Oh! Hold on," I blurt out.

He stops and turns to look at me. I run back to the open passenger door – *ow!* – and reach in to grab my phone off the arm rest. I quickly pick it up and slip it into my back pocket, then run back up to him. He doesn't turn around and start walking again. He just continues to stare at me in this odd look of… disbelief? Annoyance?

"What is that?" He inquires in a frustrated tone.

"My phone."

"Are you fucking kidding me with this?"

He closes the distance between us, grabs my arm, and turns me around.

"Hey!"

He fishes the phone out of my pocket.

"What the hell's your problem?" I protest.

He holds my phone up at the level of his face and dramatically points up at it with his other hand.

"This is how they found you! *This* is what almost got you killed!"

I hadn't considered this.

He throws it hard against the brick wall of the hardware store. It ricochets from the wall to the ground.

"It's a world-proof case. That's not gonna do anything," I mutter.

He whips the gun out of his pocket without breaking eye contact with me and puts a hole through my phone.

"Look at that. It's not *your-world*-proof."

He turns and starts walking again. I follow.

"I didn't think about the phone... I'm kind of new at this 'wanted' thing."

He briefly glances back at me over his shoulder without breaking his stride. He shakes his head huffing humorlessly.

"You're not new at it, trust me." He mumbles.

"What?"

"I said, it didn't occur to me that you could be that dumb. I'll make sure and check you for trackable devices next time.

Come on, we need to put some distance between us and here, *like now.*"

I run to catch up, clutching my throbbing wound in attempt to make it throb less. We walk down the row of cars. Suddenly, he whistles appreciatively and turns in. I look at the car he's chosen.

"Mmm's nice. Midlife crisis that someone saved up a long time for," I comment.

"Well if they saved up a long time for it, they were most likely smart enough to get insurance."

He walks up to the driver's side door and gets to work. I sigh and walk around to the passenger side and wait for him to let me in. Looking at the store entrance, I lean back on the window and stick my thumbs in my front pockets.

"Got it."

I hear the click of the lock. That was pretty quick. He must do this a lot. I open the door and sit down closing the door back up. He's already popped a panel out of the way and is working with wires under the steering wheel. The vehicle roars to life.

"Fuck." He curses and melts into his seat with dismay placing his hand longingly on the top of the steering wheel.

"What? What is it?"

"Gas is almost on empty. I don't feel like stopping to fill up. Let's go. New car." He opens the door and gets out.

I can't help but smile.

"You're such a dick," I laugh as I get out myself.

10.

Running

The new car is not quite as nice looking but it smells... actually new, like it's fresh off the lot. I kind of feel bad for whoever owned it.

I fiddle with the cuff. I hate that I can't take it off. I need to leave it alone and distract myself. Think of something else.

"Won't they have our faces now? Are police going to be looking for us?"

"Nope, it's going to be covered up because of who we are."

"And *who are we* again? I *missed* that part."

He's silent.

"Can you at least tell me who we're running from? Those last two weren't like the others..."

"Because they don't work for the same people," he interrupts. "We call them The *Activists*. They don't agree with what the government is doing, so they've started to try and take things into their own hands."

"Wait, government?" My voice is steadily getting louder "We're running from the government? That's who's after me? I'm wanted by the government?"

"Calm down, Sophie! I'm gonna get you through!"

"You can't out run the government, Kael! Not forever! And who do *you* work for?" I demand at my new heightened state of mental distress.

"The government."

"What?" I shriek pulling at the cuff like I'm trying to remove a bangle bracelet.

"It's alright! I'm not bringing you in! You *know* that!"

I stop and close my mouth to think for a moment.

So I am being hunted down by the government... *and* 'The Activists'." I use air quotes. "How does that make sense? Why did you kill those guys, then? Aren't they by default on '*our side*?'" I finish with off with air quotes again.

"Not exactly. No. They want us dead."

"Fantastic. Of course they do. I knew that. I thought you said they didn't agree with what the government is doing? And if the *government* wants me dead..."

"The government doesn't want you dead."

"But your friend?"

"They hadn't *intended* for him to die."

"What were they doing with —"

"Experimentation."

I feel like the wind has been knocked out of me. I wait for him to say more but he doesn't.

"What kind of experimentation." I almost whisper.

He sighs in defeat.

"In the last thirty-two years, government scientists have been responsible for bringing ten synthetic human beings into the world."

I stare at him, fearing where this story is going, keeping my mouth shut as to not distract him from continuing.

"These synthetics... were produced, one each year, for ten years, each slightly improved as they perfected the science." He pauses to sneak a peek at my face.

I only stare back, unblinking.

"Since these synthetics were... superior to the general population, their first role was – naturally – as a weapon. The first nine were raised together, trained to neutralize threats. The tenth one... the tenth one was different, made the same way and everything, but was supposed to be more of a study, to observe the effects of a normal life... normal upbringing. After the tenth was made, they stopped production to focus on everything they already had.

He stops speaking, the ride is silent for a moment. This isn't possible. It's not. It's crazy. Synthetic human beings? This kind of stuff doesn't exist. Maybe in the future... like, way, way in the future. But not now! Not me! This can't *be*. It's not true! It's not!

He clears his throat. "Last year there was a development in their research; it showed a distinct variation that occurred in both Nine and Ten. But when they tried to repeat it in Eleven, they couldn't. So they brought Nine in to run some tests... the tests unfortunately resulted in his death... so now they need Ten." He mutters with obvious disgust.

Horrified, I gulp air and look down at my hands folded in my lap.

"So why do they need me?" I whisper barely audible.

I already know the answer. I'm not stupid. I just want the story's ending to have a nice little plot twist that will undo all that I'm feeling right now and allow me to finally exhale the breath I've been holding since he started talking.

He looks at me with pained, apologetic blue eyes.

"I told you that knowing wouldn't make this any easier."

I push at the cuff again. Why? Why, what? I don't even know. All I keep thinking is *why*. I'm not sure how to form the question in my head. For myself. I can't say why *me?* Why did this have to happen to *me?* It's *me* because *they made me.* I can't say why did they make *me*, because that doesn't really make sense... I wish I'd never been born? Just so I wouldn't have to deal with *this?* Is that what I'm thinking? I guess that *works...* it *applies...* but it's not exactly what I'm thinking.

"Why did they do this?"

"Start with these experiments? I don't know what the 'variation' was – "

I shake my head to interrupt his air-quote.

"No, start making synthetic humans."

He puts his hand back on the wheel.

"It has to do with evolution."

"Evolution?"

"Yeah, the scientists were concerned that the human race had stopped evolving."

"What do you mean?"

He furrows his brows, gathering his thoughts.

"Evolution. First we swam up on shore. Then we grew legs. Turned into monkeys. Cavemen. Until there came the humans of today."

"We're more like *relatives* to the *chimpanzee* family, not monkeys, but alright, continue."

"Well, besides getting about two feet taller since BC we haven't evolved since then – aside from those born without pinky toes or wisdom teeth – but why did we stop? They don't know. And they figured if we stop evolving and our strained planet continues to harden, eventually we won't be strong enough for our own world, and it will do away with us. So to fight the impending extinction of our race, we must force ourselves to evolve."

"But that's not how it's supposed to be. Evolution is just supposed to happen – "

"And that's why we have the league of anti-government activist after us. You see?" He interrupts. "But what if we don't evolve on our own anymore? Are you suggesting we tie ourselves to the tracks and watch the train come? What have we got to lose by trying to push it along? We as living things... we're only fighting for our own survival."

"Why don't we just, you know, take care of the planet so that it doesn't harden and kill us?"

"They are... they're trying... but there aren't enough of them for that. *This* is something they *can* do to make a difference. So it's what they're doing."

"Creating killers from scratch."

"That was only phase one. You're the start of phase two. The plan was to insert synthetics into the general public to populate the future."

"OK? Care to elaborate a little more?" I push

"What came first? The chicken or the egg?"

"What? What does that – "

"Just answer the question." He presses

"The chicken, it evolved from something that swam out of the ocean, too."

"The egg came first. That first egg was the hybrid of whatever was laying those eggs and a mutation."

"You know, you seem to be very on board with all of this. So what are we doing? Who are we to stand in the way? We're just two people and we're talking about the future of our race... well the *human* race whether we're part of it or not."

He stops and appears to be seriously considering what I've said. It scares me a little that he might have changed his mind. I mean, I know. Morally. I'm just one person. My life is pretty insignificant in this case. But like he said, we all fight for our own survival.

"I did agree with them, until they got greedy. It was working fine, but they wanted too much too fast and they're willing to sacrifice lives to get it."

"Now it's bad that they're sacrificing lives? Funny, coming from an assassin."

"You don't betray your own! That's the one rule!"

He's upset.

We're both silent. I think he's giving me some time to myself to think. I'll take it. I have more questions, but I think he needs some time, too.

11.

Issues

The ride is completely silent for a full twenty minutes... aside from the sound of jingling as I continuously fiddle with the cuff.

"That thing's really botherin' you, huh?"

His words cut through the silence making me jump a little. I look at him and he's looking at the cuff, gesturing to it with his chin.

"I told you, I'm not going to attach you to any more car doors. If it makes you feel better, close the other one around your wrist too. So it's not dangling."

The idea makes me shudder.

"That'll make it worse. Then there'll be two."

I want the silence back. I'm kind of... in shock, I think. I didn't even know I was adopted. I have so many more questions, but at the same time, I don't want to know. I don't want to know any of this. I want things to go back to the way they were. I want to go back to yesterday and stay there. I want to redo this morning. Make stew. Go for my run. Call Frida. Listen to my music. My phone is gone now, and oddly, I really, really just wish I had it so I could listen to my music. Nice, mind numbing music. And forget the world... forget this.

"But then you wouldn't have it in your mind that you're going to be trapped somewhere again."

I sigh, he's still trying to talk to me.

"I'm already trapped. It's stuck on me. I can't get it off, it's stuck on me, I'm stuck *in* it. Therefore, I'm trapped. I feel really claustrophobic right now! OK?" I ramble, half out of my mind.

He stares at me like he's waiting for me to explain myself. It's either that, or he's confused and he can't think of a way to form his confusion into a question.

"I have... *err*... commitment issues."

The look of confusion dulls only slightly as it is joined by a look of amusement via the arching of his eyebrows and formation of a grin, which he tries, *with fail,* to conceal.

"Commitment to handcuffs?"

"Stuff like this... anything... everything. I don't know. I'm weird like that."

"What do you mean by anything and everything?"

"I mean... like... I can't even wear a *bracelet* for more than two hours... so... handcuffs? They're driving me insane right now."

I look at him with pleading eyes. The smile disappears from his mouth. He looks ahead and pulls the car over to the side of the road.

"What are you doing?" I ask.

"We're gonna get it off. I didn't know it was this big a deal. You should have told me this was a thing."

I feel a smile spread across my face as I continue to stare at him.

"I can't make things different for you, but I *can* get that cuff off your wrist."

He puts the car in park and grabs the soda can that's sitting in the cup holder.

"What's that going to do?" I ask curiously.

He whips a generously sized knife out. I didn't even know he had one on him. He stabs it into the can and carves out a rectangle. Then he takes the cut and folds it into a semi-tube. I watch quietly, thoroughly intrigued. His eyes dart to my face and he smirks. Then he takes my wrist and starts feeding the bent tin into the cuff to render the locking teeth useless.

"That's genius. I didn't think of that."

He chuckles.

"Just like you didn't think of how it's a *bad idea* to hold onto a smart phone while trying to elude the government."

I slap the back of his head with my free hand.

"Ay!" He chuckles. "Do you want this off or not?"

"For the last time! I get it! OK? It just didn't occur to me *at the time*. And in my defense, I didn't know we were running from the government at that point."

"Still applies. Everyone uses that shit now. They actually have an app for it."

"Shut up," I mumble in defeat.

He chortles some more and the metal falls from my wrist. My relief is indescribable. It's as if I can breathe now... not that I was holding my breath, but it feels like my lung capacity has improved by at least sixty percent. I take a series of deep appreciative gulps of air.

"That good?" he laughs

"Yes, thank you," I sigh, smiling happily.

"Thank you? I didn't know you could *say* that."

His playful smirk is intoxicating. Stupid, cocky... why does he have to be so frickin' adorable?

"I'm not *that* big a dick, I know when to be appreciative. Maybe *you* should strive to deserve a thank you more often."

"Maybe I *should*," he agrees.

His grin widens as he puts the car back in drive and pulls us back onto the road.

"I've only hauled your ass out of danger three and a half times now," he continues.

"Is the *half* the handcuff? Because that shouldn't count. I thanked you for that."

"No, the half was your phone."

"Seems a little desperate, including that, doesn't it?

"Nope, I don't think so, little girl."

"Don't call me little girl!"

"Well you are."

"I am *not* this vulnerable *little thing*! Just give me a weapon... like your knife or something. I'm good with knives."

"Oh no, no, no."

"What's that supposed to mean? Why the hell not?"

"You do *not* bring a knife into fight unless you know how to defend yourself against one. Understand? It's a delicate situation, and there's a good chance it's going to get taken away from you. You have to be able to deflect and retrieve."

"I've been in a knife fight before so— "

"When? *When* have you been in a knife fight?" He sputters doubtfully.

"With a mugger a year and a half ago. My best friend was there. We could call her right now if you didn't put a hole through my phone – look at this scar!" I hold up my hand to show the faded indent that stretches across my palm.

"Jesus, what did you do? Grab the blade?"

"Yes." I admit sheepishly.

"Wow, Soph, you were in a knife fight and got yourself a gorgeous scar when you almost lost the top half of your hand. Bravo!"

"Well… I won."

"Sophie, I'm not giving you *shit* until I know *without a doubt* that you're gonna be the one who's gonna walk out alive. I seem to enjoy your company for some reason."

"But that's impossible. There's *always* a chance of dying. And if we're going up against these guys, I'm gonna need something to shoot them with."

"*We...* are not. *I* am. This is what *I* do. Let me handle it. OK? All you need to remember for now is that guys don't hold up well to a kick to the balls, and biting off a finger takes the same amount of force as biting through a carrot."

"What was the pointing of keeping me alive if you're just going to stick me on the sidelines. I *want* to help. I'm *going* to help. This is my *life* now, like you said. So bring it. Train me. In a way... I've kind of been preparing for this my whole life."

He's silent, pursing his lips.

"Plus... apparently I was kind of *made* for this," I add quietly.

He looks at me, his mouth slightly agape.

"You're not getting a weapon yet," he declares.

Well, 'yet' sounds better, but I'm not five and he's not the fucking boss of me.

"Well then I'm taking my lighter back. So that I can at least singe people *and or* light a Molotov."

Before he can respond I shove my hand into his front pocket and fish around for the butane lighter.

"Woah! Hey! Jesus!" The sound of squealing wheels fills the car as he swerves a little.

I grab hold of the lighter and, in the process, bump his... man part. Oops. I pull my hand out of his pocket clutching the prize. It's my turn to smirk at *him* as *he blushes.*

"Get a little excited there, champ?"

"Shut up," he smirks, only meeting my eyes for a second before he returns his attention to the road.

"Now we're even."

"How's that?"

He's trying really hard to stop smiling.

"You got to feel me up. It's only fair I get to return the favor," I joke.

"By that logic, I think, I would need to be feeling up something more than your stomach," he smiles devilishly. "Where we gonna eat out tonight?"

"What?" I gasp

"Food. Dinner." He smirks knowingly.

"Oh, um. Nice segue." Now I'm blushing "Should we really be stopping? I mean this isn't a fun road trip for shits and giggles. We're on the run from the feds."

"This is a road trip for you? Our total driving time, not including all the stops, has only been... I don't know, *two and a half hours*? Most of which time you weren't conscious for, so it shouldn't even really count toward that total."

"Hey, I grew up in Rhode Island, alright? Anything over *twenty-eight minutes* is a road trip."

He chuckles.

"And it *is* a road trip. We're going to Nebraska, you said."

"Yeah, I'm just giving you a hard time." He looks down at my bloody shirt. "We're gonna have to do something about this before we go anywhere," he adds, pinching the material of my shirt between his fingers and giving it a gentle tug.

"How you doin' there, by the way?"

"I'm alright," I sigh sticking my finger in the hole in my shirt before lifting the fabric to look at my wound. "Just stings a little. It's fine."

"It's still bleeding." He points out then reaches into the side of his pants pulling out his knife again. "Now, you can *borrow* this to cauterize that, but I want it back before you step out of this car, deal?"

"Cauterize?"

"Yeah, it'll stop the bleeding. I'll walk you through it."

"I know how to cauterize something. I've just never actually done it before."

This is really going to hurt.

12.

Born and Raised

"OK." I say as confidently as I can manage. I take the knife from his hand and position the lighter over my lap.

"You OK?"

"Yeah I got this."

I open the knife and hold the tip of the blade over the lighter before I flick on the flame.

"You gotta hold it like that for a while, you need the knife red hot."

"Yeah, I know."

It can't be that bad. I'm pretty tolerant to pain after a lifetime of my pastimes. I can do this.

I watch the knife slowly start to glow.

"OK, that's good," Kael assures me.

I let the button go and drop the lighter into my seat.

"You ready?"

"Mhmm."

"Just lift your shirt and hold it against the opening of the cut."

"Don't I need to stick it in?" I ask quickly.

"No, it's shallow enough that this should be fine. Just do it before the knife cools down."

I quickly comply to his instruction.

"AYE-AHhmmm!"

"Hold it there for a few seconds. You're almost good."

I suck and push shallow amounts of air through my teeth as I wait for him to tell me when.

"OK, OK, that's enough."

I rip the knife away from my skin and take a deep breath.

"You alright?" he asks with a new grin.

"Yeah, yeah, I'm good. I'm good."

He chuckles in some congratulatory, welcome-to-the-club way.

"You did good."

"Now what about the shirt? I can't get out of the car in public with a bloody shirt, people will think I killed someone."

"You can use my shirt. I've got an undershirt on."

"You've got an undershirt on? And you bandaged my arm with your nasty sock?"

"Well now I *need* the undershirt, so I guess it's a good thing I went with the nasty sock."

I laugh. He's fun.

"So what do you want to eat?" he asks again.

"I don't know, what's good?"

"Well I don't know, what would you not throw out a window?"

"Ha. Just find a bar or something."

"You know, you're taking this pretty well. I mean... I thought you should know... you're not half bad at this – you know, – in a mental sense."

"Oh, so happy to have your approval! God, I don't know what I would have done without that." I smirk.

"I'm serious," he laughs. "You're all right."

"Don't congratulate me yet. It could just be shock. Give it some time to sink in. My whole life... is a lie. There's a group of people that want me dead. And the government wants to run lethal experimental tests on me, which is probably morally OK because I'm not a real person anyway, right?"

"You *are* a real person. You just weren't born the same way... you were hanging out in some tank for nine months instead of a woman's uterus. You're still made of the same stuff.

Well – kinda – for the most part. Just instead of two people's genetic makeup, you were compiled from a whole bunch of the good parts of a bunch of different people's genetic makeup... and then altered some... or a lot. I don't really know."

"You're not very good at this," I tease with a smile.

"Well someone else could tell you this and make it sound a lot more scientific, but I only know the layman's version. I'm the muscle, I'm not the brains, OK? What do you want from me?"

I snicker.

"So your friend was Number Nine," I clarify cautiously. I know the friend is a difficult topic for him.

"Yes... Gage was... Gage."

"And the other eight... synthetics... You're one of them?"

He did say he *grew up* with Number Nine. And if they were all weapons... sounds to me like they were government *hitters*. Furthermore, if he's two years older than me that would make him Number Eight.

"Smartass," he breaths with a weak smile, still trying to cover up the sorrow of his loss. "Yes, I'm *one of them*."

"So how are we superior, exactly?"

"We're more resilient. We have the ability to do everything just a little bit better, a little bit faster, a little bit longer. We're stronger; we can run faster, longer, jump farther.

Not really... observant people will just think, 'oh, that guy's *really* good,' not, 'the world is being invaded by aliens' or anything... We still have to work out to keep in shape, but we're just capable of *more* and it comes easier to us."

"Hmm."

"We're also steadier, so we have *really good* aim. Oh! We, uh... it doesn't take us long to sober up. Our bodies burn off intoxicants and drugs a lot faster, which really sucks if you're in need of pain killers. Um, we... we have a nearly impervious immune system..." He racks his brain for something else.

I don't really want to talk about this anymore right now. I want to think about something else. Anything else. This is way too much to take in.

"Can we talk about something else for a while? I just need... a break. Please?"

He looks at me, a little off balance. Like I startled him.

"Yeah. What do you wanna talk about."

"I don't know. You. Your upbringing. You grew up with nine others? Sounds *fun.*" I prompt with a little smirk and raised eyebrows.

"Yes," he hisses. "All boys. Being second youngest I learned pain tolerance, and how to fight off someone bigger than me early on. But at the same time, they didn't ever let anyone –

other than them – get the drop on me. The only one I had to worry about was Gage."

His brows furrow but he quickly shakes it off.

"So where did you grow up? Was it like a school or something?" I throw the question at him to help him distract himself.

"No," he laughs. We had a normal childhood aside from the intensive training... and knowing from the beginning what we were, what we had to become. We all went to school. We were kind of like a normal family... still are."

"Nine boys... big family. So who raised you? Did they stick you all with a super strict couple?"

"Ma, she did it by herself. Tough lady. Raised us right. Head would give her the targets and then she split up the jobs and assigned them to us."

"So when did you... start?"

"When I was eight."

"What? No! You can't. Eight years-old? No!"

"Yeah."

"No! Eight years-old? That's impossible! You can't perform an assassination at the age of eight."

"Well I didn't carry out any jobs on my *own* 'til I was thirteen."

"Thirteen's not any better! I thought you were going to say sixteen or seventeen! How could she do that?"

"She only sent us when she was sure we would succeed. And it really wasn't up to her, *someone* had to do it, she just got to decide which one of us could handle the job."

"You were eight!"

"And now I'm 24, still alive, we all are, we all made it." He pauses. Gage is gone now. "It wasn't some kid's karate classes I was taking. I was heavily trained, conditioned since before I can remember, to kill. I was *built* for it. I wasn't going to fail."

How could someone send a kid out to kill? I mean sure he wasn't just any kid but...

"So you've been a hitter for sixteen years?"

"That is correct."

"Those guys back at the house were afraid of you."

"Damn straight." He gives me another devilish smile then turns into a parking lot. "You know, you're the first person that I've ever talked to about this stuff. Well, besides my brothers. I used to imagine what it'd be like telling someone. It didn't play out so great in my head. Thanks for... not being afraid of me."

"Don't flatter yourself, terminator boy. Not much scares me," I smirk.

"I noticed. But it's more than that. You're the most *open* person I've ever met. I just met you and I feel like I've known you forever. You can just... say whatever pops into your head. *I can't get you to shut up*, and that's... something else. You were completely yourself from the moment I first saw you. You held nothing back and you didn't even trust me yet."

"Just to be clear, I still don't *actually* trust you all that much," I smile meaningfully.

"I know. That's partially what I'm trying to explain. I know you. I know how you think because you're so transparent."

"Your tone suggests I should take that as a compliment."

"It's... nice. I know it sounds nuts, but I never had that growing up. I couldn't have real friends because I couldn't tell them anything. I always had to watch what I said and did. The lies would keep building up 'til I just couldn't do it anymore. I hate lying... so much. It's the only thing I hate about this gig."

"Well, I guess *for now*, you'll have to settle with being honest with me," I mumble.

"*For now*," he smirks.

I look out the window to see where we are. Some Irish bar. Eh. This will do. He pulls into a spot and turns the car off.

"'Kay." He pulls his shirt over his head. His undershirt drags up as well revealing his toned midsection. I feel my cheeks get warm again. He pulls the shirt back down when he finishes removing the shirt he's loaning me. He holds it out to me.

"Take your shirt off."

I narrow my eyes at him. He immediately understands, scoffs and turns his head to look out the driver's side window.

"I won't look, just take it off and put this on quick, alright?"

I snatch the shirt out of his hand and place it in my lap, lining it up to pull it on fast before removing my own shirt. Tossing the bloody mess to the floor in front of me and glancing frantically from window to window, I pull his on. I really liked that shirt... Oh, the sock! The sleeve covers my arm where the sock is tied, so if I just take this off... as long as it isn't bleeding...

"OK. I'm done," I inform him as I untie the sock and check the wound. This will work. I pull the sleeve back down.

He looks back at me.

"Look at that, I get to see you in my tee shirt and I only just met you today. I already gotta worry about you stealing my clothes."

I punch him hard in the arm and he laughs. I push the door open, get out, and slam it shut before he has time to open his own door. When he emerges himself, he's still chuckling. He catches up to me quickly as I start walking to the front entrance and pulls the door open to let me go first.

"So what about you?" He asks.

"What about me?"

"Your childhood. What was it like, *miss normal life*?"

"Oh, no. I don't talk about that."

I look back at his face and his brows are furrowed.

"Why not?"

"It's really not a big deal. It's just... a while back, I decided I wasn't going to let my life be about my mother anymore. And since my childhood is like a testament to her, I don't talk about it. All you need to know is that I turned out alright," I shrug.

His eyebrows pull even closer together as I turn away and walk inside.

13.

Bad Sign

There's no one else in the bar... is that a bad sign? We make our way to the bar stools and sit down. The bartender leisurely makes his way over.

"What can I get for you guys?" he asks. This guy seems friendly enough.

"What have you got for food?" I ask.

He turns around and grabs some menus and places them in front of us.

"I'll give you a minute. Any drinks to start off?"

"Just water, please," I smile.

"Me too," Kael adds.

The man nods his head and starts to turn, then stops and faces us again, looking intently at Kael. Shit! I knew our faces would be on the news with a big fat 'wanted' all over them!

"What happened to your...?" He gestures to his own face drawing an invisible line under his eye.

Phew! Thank god! Damn, this is nerve racking. Is this how Kael feels all the time? Probably not, he's too relaxed. Maybe when he first started... when he was eight years-old.

"I punched him in the face," I blurt.

A grin immediately spreads across the bartender's face as he lets out a short cackle. I look at Kael who's staring at me already with his mouth agape in disgust.

"She got'cha good, man," he laughs.

"Yup, she's a rough one," Kael utters, not looking away from me.

Kael's gawk morphs into a glare and turns to the man behind the bar. Immediately, he stops laughing and walks away. Kael turns his attention back to me. I can't wait to hear what he has to say.

"I was – " He's interrupted by a buzzing.

A phone? What? Why can *he* have a phone? He pulls a phone out of his back pocket and looks at the screen a bit too long before pressing the answer button. He hesitates for a moment gritting his teeth then places it to his ear.

"Yeah."

"The fuck is wrong with you!" A woman's voice screeches from the phone loud enough for me to hear. "I raised you to be fuckin' smart'a than this! The fuck are you doin' goin' up against Head? Don't you dare make me lose anoth'a baby! Don't you dare, Kael! You bring that girl – "

"Ma! Would you calm down, please?! Hold on a sec!"

He pulls the phone away from his ear and clutches it to his chest practically jumping off his stool. I suppress a giggle at the sight of his obvious distress.

"*Stay here*. Don't move," he tells me.

He starts walking toward the restroom. Halfway there, he looks back giving me a quick nod as he places the phone back to his head.

She sounds worried... like a real mother... well, she did raise him. She clearly cares about his well-being. I really don't know what to make of his upbringing. But at the same time it seems like it must have been exciting. Nine hot-headed boys and a single mother.

The bartender returns placing two waters in front of me. "You know what you want to order, little lady? Or do you want me to come back when your friend returns?"

I grimace at his endearment but quickly wipe it off my face before he can process the perturbed expression.

"Well actually... can I just have scrambled eggs?"

"I can do that," he chuckles. "Wouldn't want to get *you* mad."

I smile and give him a little laugh. He smiles warmly and walks away. I take a sip of water.

I hear the door open and turn to see a guy with perfect hair walk in. OK, so other people *do* come to this bar. He notices me looking at him and flashes me a big cocky white smile, then runs a hand through his hair and winks. I roll my eyes and scoff before turning back around and inspecting the bottles of alcohol on the shelves. He sits at the other end of the bar and wave at the bartender who walks over to him and starts up a conversation that I don't care to listen to.

It's nearly dark now. Dad is probably home. Home to a smashed in door and dead bodies all over the place. I need to call him. Let him know I'm OK. What will I tell him? Does he know what I am? Does he know what's going on? Has he been keeping me in the dark all my life? Does he *not* know? At this point, it would be *easier* if he knew... I don't want to have to tell him. I don't have the answers myself. But at the same time, if he knows, I'm gonna be fucking pissed.

A glass is placed down on the bar and slid closer to me. I turn and look at the asshole who's about to hit on me.

"No thanks," I say before he can speak.

"I just thought you could use some company. Saw you sitting here all by yourself and figured, why else go to a bar other than to meet new people?"

Oh, this guy sounds way too smooth. It's unnerving.

"Not up for meeting any more new people today, sorry."

"OK, OK." He puts his hands up in surrender... it reminds me of Kael earlier... I hope he's almost done on the phone. I should use his phone to call Dad.

"You seem like you could use a drink... seem a little tense."

Ugh! Is this guy still trying?

"Nope, I'm good. Not interested in your drink *or* your company." I look at the restroom arch. "Look, I'm here with someone, so..." I look back at him and he seems closer. His arm is outstretched across the bar.

"Hey that's cool. I'll just keep you company till he gets here, huh?"

Is this guy for real? I mean seriously. *What?*

"Look, I'm done being nice, alright? I'm only going to say this once. Go. The fuck. Away. But I'll tell you what, it's completely up to you if you wanna see what happens in about five seconds if you don't comply."

"I'd listen to her, Patrick," the bartender interjects. "You should'a seen the other guy."

Mr. Ass-Wipe puts his hands back up where the bartender can see them, stands up from Kael's stool and backs away. I watch him take his seat back at the other end of the bar before I turn back to face the bartender.

"Thanks," I smile.

"Don't worry about it, kid," he smiles back, placing a plate of scrambled eggs in front of me.

"You got any ketchup?"

"Sure, I got ketchup." He reaches under the bar returning his hand with a red bottle. "Whole bottle." He takes the packaging off and places it on the side of my plate.

"Thanks so much."

He nods still smiling warmly, and starts to turn away.

"One more thing, sorry"

He turns back.

"Do you know where I can find a phone?"

Kael is taking too long. And he's probably going to give me a hard time about using his anyway.

"When you walk outside to the left, there's a phone booth not far from the door."

"Thanks. I'm gonna leave this here. I *will* be back. Please don't clean it up," I tell him, circling my index finger above my plate of eggs.

"No problem. It'll be here when you get back." He winks as he's finally able to return to his other duties.

I stand, take a big gulp of my water and place the glass back next to my eggs. Hmm... the ice must be melting. It tastes kinda gross now. I turn on my heel and head for the door. It's dark. The street lights are on, conveniently illuminating the phone booth.

I take my first step out into the night. I feel different all of the sudden, like I just had five shots of tequila or something. What the heck? I step again trying to shake this off. The *hell* is going on? I cross the lot. The impairment I'm feeling is really starting to scare me and Kael's eyes are so pretty. I just can't get over how pretty they are. Ooo, here's the phone! That's what I need! I pick it up and place it to my ear.

"Hello?"

I giggle to myself, that's not right... I need to dial first. But wait... there's no sound. Why isn't it working? Stupid phone! I put it back on the hook and try it again. Still no sound. What is wrong with this thing? Why won't it work? OH! I know! I need to pay. I need money... I have no money... maybe Kael will give me some money. I don't want to ask Kael for money. I can do this myself. I make my own money. I can pay with my own money. But I don't have any... and I need some... I can pay him back. I'm good for it. He'll believe me. I know he will. Who wouldn't believe *me*?

"Hey love, phone trouble?"

Oh, it's the guy that was trying to talk to me before...

"Oh, yes. It won't work. I need money... but I don't have any."

"That's a shame. Did you need someone to come pick you up?"

"Um," do I? I guess so. That would work. Yeah, I need to get home... to talk to my Dad. I need to tell him – "

"Well, you're in luck. 'Cause I would *love* to take you home."

"Really?"

"Absolutely."

He comes over to me to help me walk. How did he know walking is such a feat all of the sudden? He must be really smart.

"But you... you don't know where I live. It's really far. *Two and a half hours!* Kael said that's not long. But *I* said it *was.*"

"Oh, no, yes, it is, you are absolutely right, it is. But that's OK. I'll take you."

We're walking, we must be going to his car. That makes sense.

"That's *so* great, you mean it?"

"I do."

"But wait! My eggs! I have to eat my eggs I told him to leave them there!"

"We can get you some new eggs."

"But that's wasteful. He made them for me. Special! They weren't even on the menu!"

I push his hands away. Ooo... wobbly. What's happening. Something is bad. Something feels very bad. It must be because of the eggs, I can't waste the eggs, I need to go eat the eggs. The bartender was so nice to make them for me, the least I can do is eat them. I walk for the door.

"Wait, wait, wait."

His hand is back on me. Stopping me. I don't like it.

"No! I don't like the touching!"

"Aw, you don't mean that."

He's holding me tighter. He turns me to face him. This is not right. This is bad. *He's* what's bad. I ball my free hand up into a fist and shoot it at his face. He let's go and grabs his nose with both hands.

"*I said* I don't like it!"

"UGH! Bitch!" He removes his hands from his face. There's red everywhere. "You broke my friggin' nose!"

Where's Kael... I want Kael.

"Kael?" I walk for the door.

"Hey, hey, hey." He grabs my arm. "You're not going anywhere!" He yanks and I lose my balance, falling back into his arms.

"Get off!" I shout.

"Shut up!"

"Kael!" I call louder.

He has my biceps pinned to my sides and he's dragging me backwards. I wriggle and stomp on his foot. His grip loosens slightly. I use the opportunity to slide to the ground, spread my feet and close them around one of his feet then roll over dropping him to the ground. As quickly as I can in this dazed state, I get to my feet and kick him in the side steadying myself with my outstretched arms. Once he cries out in pain I know it's safe to assume I can do it again without much chance of him catching my foot. I swing again, more agonized shouts fill the air.

Satisfied, I turn around to walk back inside the bar, but my ankle is yanked backward and the ground races up. I catch myself weakly with my forearms. Not enough to keep my forehead from crashing against the asphalt, but enough keep me from blacking out. I grab my head with both hands and roll over onto my back. My wrists are ripped away from my face and I'm lifted to my feet, then raised higher than that. Over his shoulder.

"Stupid fucking bitch," he mutters. "Fucking hurt! You're gonna pay for that."

The Earth sways around upside down slightly blurred as he trudges forward with an obvious limp. A shine catches my eye. I knife sticking out of his back pocket. A butterfly knife. I know the model, I can tell from the design used to skeletonize the handles and the slightly thicker latch suggesting that it's spring loaded. They stopped making these a while back. I never could get one. This guy either has connections and a lot of money, or he's one of the lucky people who got his hands on one before it was discontinued.

"Do you have any idea who I am?"

"Doesn't' matter," I wince. "You're fucking dead."

I reach down, grab the knife out of his pocket, squeeze the handles together to open the latch, and flick my wrist around to secure the blade in its exposed state. I plunge it into his back.

He stops. Arches back. Falls forward, on top of me, writhing in pain. His face expresses terror as he visibly clutches to the life rapidly leaving him. I scramble back, out from beneath him and crawl further back to put some distance between me and him, his eyes follow me. I watch as he slows to a stop. His eyes go suddenly... blank.

Fuck... fuck wha'did I do? Wha'did I do?

I had to do it. I tried to walk away. I didn't want to, he made me do it. I had to. It was him or me. No one's going to believe me, I'm going to jail... he's fucking dead!

No.

I crawl forward and grasp the knife, yank it out and fall back again. I stare at it in my hand. This is evidence. I have to keep it so they don't find it. I close it up and stick it in my back pocket.

Come on get up. Get up. You need to get out of here.

I look at the body again and slowly rise to my feet. I turn away from it and walk for the door again. Nothing stopping me this time.

14.

Sorry

When I get inside the bartender sees me and stares, his mouth agape.

"You OK, kid?"

I nod once and continue walking, making my way for the men's room.

I push open the door.

"Kael?"

He's pacing in front of the urinals.

"Hold on, Sophie... No, Ma!"

He sees me while he's turning for another round across the tiled floor and stops in his tracks. All of a sudden, he's full on staring at me.

"I gotta go, Ma." Before she could have responded he hangs up the phone and sticks it in his back pocket. "What the fuck happened?"

"I don't know... I feel really weird." I press my hand to my forehead.

In two steps he's standing in front of me. He grabs my hand from my forehead.

"What happened to your face?"

I look at the hand he took and see all the blood. I wipe my forehead just above my eyebrow with the back of my free hand and pull it away to look at it. It's *a lot* of blood.

He moves on to look at my bloodied knuckles.

"Sophie, what happened? I've only been in here for, like... how did you manage to...?"

"He wouldn't let go. I told him no touching. I gave him fair warning." I wag the index finger of my blood soaked hand.

His whole expression changes and he lets go of me to clutch his hip.

"What are you talking about, *who* touched you?"

"He wanted to give me a ride home 'cause I had no money for the phone outside and I *really* want to sit down now."

I back up to the wall where I slide to the floor."

"Are you *drugged*? Did someone *drug* you?"

Hey you know... That would actually explain a lot.

105

"Yeah, I think so." I close my eyes and rest my head against the wall. "I just wanna sit here for a bit OK? It's nice and cold, and my head feels really... weird and... can you make sure there's no more... I don't want any more of that right now, OK...? I just... I just wanna sit here."

"Where is he?"

"He's in the parking lot"

"Alright listen to me. You just stay right here for a minute."

"NO." My eyes shoot open. "Just stay. OK? I just need a minute. Just give me a minute. Don't go anywhere."

"I just gotta take care'a something – "

"He's dead, Kael!"

He stares down at me.

"I stabbed him."

I lean forward, pull the butterfly knife out of my back pocket, and hold it out so he can see it. Then I drop my hand to the floor and the metal handle clinks on the tile.

Slowly he steps to the wall beside me, leans against it as I had, and slides down to my level.

He slides the knife out from under my hand.

"Here, let me hold onto that for you." His voice is soft and soothing.

I rest my head on his shoulder.

"If it makes you feel better, I was heading out to kill him myself."

"I figured."

"We've gotta go. Someone's going to call the cops. They're gonna show up… and we can't be here when that happens."

"Why? It was self-defense. I can just explain what – "

"They will arrest you and take you in for questioning."

"That's what I'm saying, I can just tell – "

"Do you remember what I said about the government making this kind of stuff go away because of who we are?"

"Yeah, but – "

"Going down to the police station is a good way for them to pick you up."

"Kael – "

"I don't want to have to hurt anyone who doesn't deserve it. Cops are just doing their job, but I have to do what I have to do."

I don't like the way that sounds.

"OK."

"OK?"

"Yeah, let's go."

I pick my head up off his shoulder.

"OK c'mon." He quickly springs to his feet, turning around to take my arm and help me up. He pulls me to my feet and we go. He walks to the door without taking his eyes off me.

"You alright?" He asks.

I nod yes and he pushes out of the bathroom. I round the corner without looking up from the floor and end up crashing into his back. Why did he stop? I hear a loud *chick chick.* I look around Kael but stays behind.

"You killed my brother's kid!" The bartender sobs behind the double barreled shotgun. "He was just a kid!"

"Whoa there. Easy buddy. Why don't you just lower the gun and we can talk about this."

"He was gonna be a cop! Just like his dad! An officer of the law!"

"Do you know what your officer of the law was doing out there? Huh?"

"Move out of the way boy!"

"Not a chance. Hey, I get it. You're looking out for yours. But I'm looking out for mine. I'm giving you a choice here. Walk away."

The gun clicks. He panics and looks at his weapon. Jammed. Kael sails across the room in a millisecond, rips the gun away from the bartender, and bashes him in the head with it.

"Kael!" I gasp in horror.

"He's fine, I just knocked him out. C'mon, let's go. We gotta get out of here."

I stay frozen where I stand staring at the man on the floor.

"Soph!"

His shout makes me jump, but it knocks me out of my paralysis. I run forward toward the entrance. Kael is already there. I stop as I'm about to pass the man.

"I'm sorry," I whisper.

"Soph, c'mon!" Kael calls again.

I run to and through the door behind Kael.

15.

Self Defense

The car is silent. It has been for 20 minutes. But I can sense Kael Is just waiting for the right amount of silence to pass before he can bomb me with questions.

"Are you ready to talk about it?"

Oh, wonderful, here it comes.

"Not really, no."

"Did he…?"

"No."

He breathes, immediately more relaxed. "Well that's a good start." I feel him look at me but I keep my eyes forward.

"But Sophie," he goes on. "It wasn't a fair fight. You pulled through. *Somehow* you pulled through."

I look at him.

"I know you *feel* guilty," he continues. "That's normal. But it was self-defense."

He looks forward to the road but I keep my eyes trained on his side profile.

"Are we doing the right thing?" My mutter is just reaching audible.

His gaze shoots back to me.

"Running away?" I elaborate.

He just continues to stare for a moment. Then he looks forward again.

"Self-defense." He answers.

16.

Complications

My phone buzzes in my pocket. Quickly, I answer it before it can disturb Sophie's sleep. I didn't even get to check to see who it was, 'cause I was watching her.

"Yeah," I say into the phone as quietly as I can manage while making sure whoever it is can still hear me.

"Kael, hey, I've got news. It's big," Luca tells me.

Oh good, I got a hold of him. I can tell him we're coming.

"Yeah? Me too. You first."

I glance back at Sophie to make sure I haven't woken her.

"Gage is alive!"

A moment passes as I process his words. They don't make sense. What did he just say? How long has it been since he spoke? Say something, Kael. He just said that Gage is alive.

"What?"

The blood drains out of my face. Gage is alive? I pull the car over, hardly off the road.

"Hold on," I instruct as I open the door and step out into the night.

I close the door quietly and take a few steps from the car.

"What are you talking about? Why would they tell us he's dead?"

"Who the fuck cares? He's alive!"

"How do you know that for sure? They could be lying. What proof do we have?"

"Do you really want to fuck around with this man? What proof do we have that he's *not* alive? Ma says you've got the girl. This works out. We can trade her in for Gage. Where are you now?"

Say something, Kael. *Say something, Kael!*

"No."

"What... what do you mean, *no?*"

"We can't give her to them."

"Like hell we can't! This is Gage! She's our only bargaining chip!"

"No. No, I'm not going to let you do that. I'm sorry, but we have to figure out something else."

"Kael, what the fuck is wrong with – "

I hang up the phone before he can finish.

No, no, no, no, fuck... Well, we're not going to Nebraska anymore. I have to come up with some other way to get Gage out or they're all going to be coming after us. Using Sophie as leverage is a good plan. The only plan. It would probably work. What the fuck am I gonna do? I can't tell Sophie they're coming after us, she'll freak. She knows what they are, she'll lose faith in me. And I wouldn't blame her. I haven't done a spectacular job so far. I look in the car. She's still sleeping soundly clutching her abdomen and most likely either reliving the traumatic events she's endured *so far,* or dreaming up what traumatic events *tomorrow* and the *next day* will bring. How can I protect her by myself? I need help. I bring my palm to my eyes and slide it down to cover my mouth and exhale harshly through my nose. *Fuck... what am I gonna do?*

17.

Bandages and Eggs

Why am I so comfortable? I open my eyes and take in my surroundings.

I'm in a bed, covered in blankets. I sit up and look around. Kael is sitting on the floor resting against a window that takes up the whole wall. He's asleep. I push the blankets away. I'm still in all the clothes I was in the last time I checked. But my stomach is itchy. I lift my shirt. My stab wound is bandaged up with gauze. Better than a sock. Speaking of... I check under my sleeve. My arm is bandaged too. I slide my legs off the bed and plant my feet on the floor. The second I push off the bed and apply pressure to the floor, Kael's eyes pop open and his head shoots up.

"Hey," he greets me, too quickly.

"Morning... I think." I look out the window to the world outside.

Not early morning... but it doesn't look like it's too far into the day either. Maybe around 10:30, give or take a half hour... probably give.

"How ya feelin?" he asks, a little more awake.

"Fine... where are we?"

He stands up.

"My place." He starts to walk toward me. "Got big plans today."

"Oh?"

"I'm gonna teach you some stuff."

He stops a few feet away, nods, then heads for the door a little way to my left.

"Really?" I chirp. "Right now?"

"Right now. Well... come on, let's get some food first."

I give the room one last look over. It's very... empty, and white. Simple. The ceiling to floor window is truly the focal point. It's beautiful... we're by the water, the view is gorgeous. I can see some small boats off in the distance.

"You comin, girly?"

"Ew, don't call me that." I grimace.

I turn and follow him out of the room. This place is so open. High ceilings. Empty except for A couch, a counter, more window, kitchen cabinets and a fridge. It's actually quite beautiful in its simplicity.

"You don't have a TV?" I ask, surprised.

"The whole window's a TV. I'll show you some time, it's pretty awesome. Interactive window. But right now, we got shit to do. Eggs?"

I look at the window again. The window is a TV?

"Yeah eggs sound good," I answer, a little preoccupied with my gawking.

I hear him open the fridge and steal my eyes from the glass. I walk over to join him in the kitchen.

"Why don't you let me." I take the egg carton from his hand.

"Don't think I can cook?"

"I make them better." I narrow my eyes playfully at him.

His mouth twitches. Cooking is something I enjoy doing, it relaxes me, and right about now, I need some normalcy. I walk around him and open up the fridge again. It's not horribly stocked. Milk. Tomatoes. I can use those. I pile it into my hands and close the door with my foot.

"Bowl, pan, and olive oil please."

I approach the stove and put my ingredients on the counter beside me.

"Here you go, ma'am."

He places my demands beside the eggs.

"Ma'am me again, and I will cook *you* instead." I press my open hand on his chest and give him a gentle warning shove.

"You wouldn't do that," he challenges. "You *need* me."

"Not *that* much," I smile.

After opening the egg carton, I position the bowl on the counter. Placing the pan on the stove, I turn my attention to the tomato. I pick up the fruit and bring it to the sink to rinse it.

"Where are the knives?"

"I don't think I should tell you," he chuckles.

I turn and threaten him with my eyes.

"Right in here."

He reaches into a drawer, still chortling, and pulls out a knife, then goes into another drawer and pulls out a cutting board. He places the board on the counter and turns to me with the knife. I shake the water off the tomato and walk over to him. Instead of letting me have the knife when I reach for it, he takes the tomato and places it on the cutting board. I can't help smiling myself as he starts chopping and I take my place at the counter beside him to crack six eggs into the bowl. He takes his chopped tomato in his hands and plops it into the egg. I splash in some milk and start going through the drawers until I find a fork to beat the eggs. Kael turns on the stove and retrieves a spatula.

I dump the contents of the bowl into the pan and go for the spatula in Kael's hand. He raises his hand high so I can't reach it.

"Their gonna burn," I warn, pulling on his arm.

He turns so that his back is to me. I climb up on his back to try and reach the spatula. But as I'm hanging by his neck with one arm and reaching up with the other, he lowers it into the pan and moves the eggs around. I slide down and drop to the floor.

"Fine," I utter, "you can stir it."

He says nothing, just laughs. I see the salt and pepper on the counter a little way away. I walk over and snatch them up. When I turn around, I discover Kael had been watching my ass. His eyes shoot back up to eye level as he tries to write it off. I narrow my eyes and shake my head.

"I saw that," I smirk.

"Saw what?" He asks innocently flashing me his bright grin.

"Mmhm," I mutter, shaking the seasonings into the pan. "Where are the plates and silverware?"

He points and I follow his finger around. I get the plates, then a pair of forks, and place it all on the counter. Kael lifts the pan over one of the plates and slides half the eggs in, then the rest into the second. I pick up a fork, dig into the one he just finished filling, and put it in my mouth.

"Well?"

"My involvement in the preparation is evident."

"You're such a smartass," he complains elatedly.

He picks up his plate and shoves a couple bites into his mouth.

"Hurry up with that, we gotta go."

"Nevada?" I whine. "I thought you said you were gonna..."

"I am, relax we're going to a paintball arena, and we're not going to Nevada anymore. There's been a change of plans."

"What's the change?" I quickly press.

"Never mind that right now. I'm gonna teach you how to handle a gun fight."

That actually sounds... fun.

"Cool." I chime and shovel in the rest of my eggs.

Kael smiles and finishes his eggs as well.

18.

Mothers

"So this place we're going, are there going to be a lot of people?"

"No, I'm gonna rent out the whole place. It's just gonna be you and me. The arena's awesome. It's all indoor, but it looks like the middle of the woods, they go all out, with the lighting, fifty-foot fake trees that stretch from floor to ceiling, and they cover the floor with leaves from outside, boulders, small caves, it's *really* elaborate. Only thing is, it's not actually *paint*ball, it's water – but we've always referred to it as paintball, so," he shrugs.

"Won't that cost a lot?"

"Money is not an obstacle. The government pays well per hit."

"They pay you?"

"Course, why else would I come to work? I need to eat *and* feed my weapon fancy – then there's my material needs. Every dangerous job has its perks. You want loyalty, you pat the dogs and keep 'em happy." His tone got real bitter by the end so I can only assume he's thinking about Gage again. I scramble for a new topic.

"How many people have you killed?"

"Seven-hundred-fifty-three."

He didn't even pause... he didn't grimace... he just kept his eyes on the road and gave me the number like it meant absolutely nothing. Seven-hundred-fifty-three?

"Seven-hundred-fifty-three? Is that all? Is that including those guys at my house and at the hardware store?"

"Oh wait no, not the last two. So, seven-hundred-and-fifty-five."

I turn and I stare at him.

"Seven-hundred and fifty-five? Seven-hundred! And fifty-five! Kael, that's like a small town!"

How can I be so at ease with this guy! He's killed seven hundred and fifty-five people!

"Well, they weren't all in the states. Terrorist groups. Threats United States citizens never got a chance to hear about... to fear."

"Don't you feel bad about it? At all?"

"Sophie, I've been at this for a long time. I passed the brooding stage a long time ago. Eventually, you have to accept and get past it."

I scoff.

"This is my *purpose*. This is what I was *made* for."

"So that's how you live with it? *They're* the ones pulling the trigger, not you?"

"If I don't pull the trigger because I'm worried about what it means for *me*, then people die. Innocent people. That's selfish. What would you have me do?"

I sigh in defeat and look away.

"That's just... a lot of people..." I mumble.

We're both silent for a couple minutes before I decide it's time for a new topic.

"So what did your mother say on the phone yesterday?"

"As much as was expected. She thinks I'm suicidal. I assured her that's not the case."

"Then what was your plan? Your original plan. After you shot me."

"I was gonna hop the states. Find myself an island somewhere. Settle down. I could handle whatever they threw at me if they ever found out where I was."

"What about your responsibility? What happened to your *if you don't pull the trigger innocent people die* speech?"

"That's why I did my job. *When* I did my job. *But they crossed a line.* Now I'm looking to quit and they can find a new solution to take my place. *I'm done.*"

We're both silent again.

"Hey, speaking of mothers – "

Oh no. I knew this would happen.

"No."

"What you said at the bar, before – "

"No, Kael. It doesn't matter. *Nothing about it* is worth addressing. Because I got through it. Would I change it if I could? No. Because *I made it through*. It made me who I am. And I *like* who I am. I can count on one hand the number of times anyone has seen me cry. I'm not afraid of *anything*. I *like* who I turned into. I wouldn't wish my childhood on anyone. It was dark and unfortunate. But my mother had... has serious depression. She spent her whole life complaining about her childhood. You know what it got her? Worse depression. She was miserable. And if *she* was miserable, she made damn sure everyone around her was, too. Or at least she would try. Me and my brother learned to laugh it off. It's why we're so thick skinned and cynical… traits I'm also OK with possessing. And what it all comes down to is that I'm *happy*. And she can't take that away. Not even by *haunting my memory*."

He stares straight ahead for a long minute not saying anything. Finally, he sighs his defeat.

"Just tell me she didn't hurt you."

"She didn't hurt me," I sigh, "she just… she ran away. At first it was just from her *responsibilities*. She wasn't a mother to me or my brother, it was more like *I* was *hers*. And then not too long ago, she ran away for real."

He is silent for a minute.

"If you ever want to talk more about – "

"Thanks for the thought… really. But I'm fine," I smile sincerely. "Besides, you had less of a childhood than I did."

"I really didn't lack a childhood. Ma packed our lunches, put us on the bus, made pancakes on Saturday mornings, and was there to talk to. We just grew up considering ourselves super heroes. It was like we lived in a comic book."

"Super heroes?"

"Yeah, killing the bad guys and saving innocent people. What else does a kid call that?"

"Well the heroes usually arrest the bad guys. Not kill them."

19.

Guerilla Warfare

When we pull into the parking lot of the paintball arena, I take notice of all the cars. I'm going to have to bribe this guy with a lot of money to clear these people out.

"So how's this going to work? There's already a bunch of people here," Sophie points out.

"In my life I have found that there are very few things that money can't fix."

I back into a spot and turn off the car. Sophie unbuckles herself and gets out. I open my door and climb out as well. We walk to the front door and I open it, letting her go in first. I take a quick glance around behind me before following her into the building.

"Oh no, no, not today, Hues!" The arena owner fumes.

"Frank – " I whine as I walk up to the desk. Soph hangs back.

"No! I got in trouble with Lidia last time. You know how many people I got out there today? It's a Saturday for Christ sake!"

"Lidia got mad? Thought she likes us?

"She did, till you screwed us out of money," he sighs.

"Screwed you out of money?"

"She said we could'a made a lot more money if you guys hadn't had me pull everyone out so you could have the place to yourselves."

"I promise I'll make it worth your while this time, and tell Lidia I'm sorry," I pull my hundreds out and unfold them. I count out nine, separate them from the stack, and slap them on the counter.

Frank looks at them, says nothing, then looks up at me. Still saying nothing, his eyes glance at the stack in my hand then back at me.

I sniff, pull three more hundreds out of my stack, and add them to the stack on the counter.

He picks up the bribe and I fold what's left of my money and stick it back in my pocket.

"And you only get two hours," he states sternly, pointing at me with his stack of hundreds.

"Fine, whatever," I sigh.

"Where do you get all this fuckin' cash anyway? You sell drugs?"

"Nah man, I'm a pimp," I smirk.

Frank just looks at me like he's considering that I might have told the truth. Then he looks at Sophie at the other end of the room. Oh *hell* no. I raise my eyebrows at him and his eyes are instantly back on me. I reach over the counter and snatch one of the hundreds back from him.

"That was a joke, Frank. I'm really a hitman for the mob so how bout you call those people out, before I lose my patience."

"So where do we start." Sophie inquires gleefully.

She's so excited I can't stop smiling. There's just something about this girl.

"Do you know how to load the gun?"

"Yeah, it's just a paintball gun, forget this. I've loaded shotguns, rifles, AK's. Just tell me what I need to do in terms of your *lesson plan.*"

"Jesus, what have you been in a war?"

"I've been around guns for a long time. Been shooting since I was little. My dad's a cop – I told you that – he got me a job at a firing range working for his old army buddy. I know how to handle a gun."

"You work at a shooting range? You are just full of surprises, aren't you?"

"Well... worked. I don't know what's happening now. I doubt I'll be going in tomorrow... which reminds me, I should probably let him know. Can I see your phone? I should really call my dad, too."

She steps toward me.

"Eh, eh, eh. No – " I raise my hand to stop her from approaching me. "Later, you're busy right now."

I give her a smirk. She stops in her tracks.

"I'm going to give you a ten second head start and then I'm coming after you."

"What is this hide and seek? You haven't taught me anything yet."

I close my eyes.

"Ten"

"Kael!"

"What's' a' matter Soph? Scared? Nine."

"I'm not scared. I just don't know what you want me to do."

"Just act instinctively. This is just to give me an idea of what I'm dealing with. Eight."

She sighs, exasperated.

"Don't worry, I'll be gentle," I smirk devilishly keeping my eyes closed.

I feel the pinch of the paint pellet spat on my chest.

"Seven." My grin widens. "You're wasting time."

"I was acting instinctively," she says innocently.

Ooo that witty playfulness is one of the reasons I *so* like this girl.

"Four." I count louder to further dramatize my skip over two numbers.

Rustling of leaves and twigs signal her retreat. Oh, if she's going to be that loud, this is going to be too easy.

"Three."

I still hear her fading into the distance.

"Two."

I can't hear her anymore.

"One."

I open my eyes and walk in the direction I heard her footsteps plunder down. There are actually drag marks in the leaves, creating a path. Oh god, I have so much work to do. I continue to follow the path until suddenly, it stops. There are no more visible clues as to where she is. I look around. She's nowhere in sight. Maybe I didn't give her enough credit. There appears to be a method behind her actions. Now to find out what the plan is before she can finish the execution. I take note of all the closest trees. I look up into the branches. Damn, where the fuck did she go?

Is there someone else in the arena with us? Did someone snatch her up? Shit! I gotta find her! Splitting up was a bad idea.

"Soph! You alright?"

I hadn't considered anything could go wrong with this plan. The splat of a pellet impacts the back of my neck. I grab my neck and spin around to the sound of her devilish chuckle. Where did that come from? I scan the strategically arranged pseudo world before me. Nothing. Then the muzzle of a paint riffle presses to my temple.

"Bang," Sophie utters triumphantly. "Underestimation is something I can use quite well. I *own* Guerrilla Warfare. Do you think this is my first time playing paintball? Stop going easy on me and treat me like a threat!"

I grab the gun and push it up holding it above my head as I step toward her. Then I pull it down to my side and yank her into me. She was ready for it, sending her elbow into my face. At least that's where it was headed before I ducked. She flails freeing her gun from my grasp and backs away. I begin to circle her. She keeps her eyes on me putting more distance between us. I lunge forward. She turns her gun around clutching it by the firing end then she swings it at me like a baseball bat. My arm shoots up automatically to block.

"Forget you've got a gun?" I chuckle.

"The bullets don't slow you down," she shrugs.

"Adaptive," I nod in agreement.

She grabs the gun by its opposite ends and rushes into me, holding the weapon out in front of her. I grab the middle with one hand, swing her around, and let go. The second she hits the ground she rolls farther away and jumps to her feet, aiming her gun at me. Seems like as good a time as any to pull my weapon. I take the paint pistol out of my pants behind my back and aim it at her. She instinctively hunches down lower and brings her arms in tighter.

"What now?" I prompt.

"Shoot and run?"

"You can see where it brings us," I grant.

She fires. I try to duck out of the way but her bullet impacts my shoulder. She takes off. I fire. Hitting her upper back. She spins around and fires again without halting her retreat, getting me square in the chest. I smile watching her continue on her path. She's fast. I start to chase after her. She giggles up ahead and I feel my grin widen further. She disappears behind a giant boulder.

I round the boulder from the opposite side. I figure she'll try to escape around this way. She's probably banking on the idea that I went the way she went. I walk all the way around without any luck. I jump up on top of the rock to check the opposite side. She's gone. Damn. Where did she go? I hop back down.

I hear the snap of a twig and twist, grabbing the gun again before it impacts the side of my head. I pull it from her and toss it away. Her foot is next. I deflect. Now the opposite foot. Spinning back kick. I step aside and let her foot pass by before grabbing her ankle and pushing up. She falls back into a roll and she's back to her feet.

She circles to the right and attempts a right hook to my face. Always the face with her! I catch her hand and swing her back into the boulder behind me, catch her other rapidly approaching hand and trap her there. She glares up at me, breathing hard. Suddenly her expression changes. A look I haven't seen in her before. She regains control of her breathing. I continue to look down at her, holding her gaze. Her face so close to my own. Those big deep dark brown eyes, her flawless face. *Get it together, man. This is not good. It was way too easy to trap her under your weight. She needs to be able to get out of this position.*

I back my face away slowly and breathe.

"Not good enough," I sigh.

Sophie's eyes morph into the very meaning of determination and she shoots her forehead into mine.

"Ah! Christ!" I utter bobbing away and grabbing my head with my right hand.

With her free hand she pushes into my left wrist freeing her other hand. Without letting go of my left hand she drops to the ground pulling my head into the boulder as she swings through my legs, smashing my crotch with my own arm on the way. She then jumps to her feet behind me and pushes me face first into the boulder, holding me there with her body weight with my arm twisted behind my back.

"Take it back." She demands.

"Alright, alright! I give!" I chuckle.

She gives me an abrupt shove and lets go. I turn around and work my arm around in a circular motion. She's smiling triumphantly at me with her arms crossed in front of her chest.

"What's next?"

"How are you so decent at this?"

"*Decent.*" She snorts. "Well for one you're still going easy on me, and two, I took lots of martial arts classes growing up."

"Ah, makes sense now."

"We gotta talk about this going easy, though."

"Well, I don't want to hit you."

"I noticed, but you kind of have to."

"I don't want you to get hurt – "

"Bruises go away," she blurts impatiently.

She *does* need to learn and there's no one else here to do it.

"We'll get to that, alright? One step at a time. I have *no doubt* that you can take a beating, but let's not worry about that yet, OK? Let's go shoot some targets."

She exhales her exasperation, then raises her hands in defeat.

"So what do you like to do on a day you're not hiding from the federal government?" I ask.

She finishes loading more balls into her gun and looks at up at me, then refocuses her eyes forward.

"Working, or these days, rock climbing at a place in Lincoln." She answers half-heartedly with her attention clearly on her aim.

She fires. Bullseye.

"Rock climbing. Sounds fun, what got you into that?"

"I was looking for a new hobby since both my brother *and* my best friend left the state to start their lives."

"That sucks."

"Nah, s'all right," she mumbles.

"Where'd they go?"

"Bruce is earning extra college credits in Orlando, and Frida is attending an art school in New York."

"So where does Bruce go to school?"

"MIT."

"Damn, he must have quite the brain."

"Yeah, he's really smart."

"What's he going for?"

"Robotic engineering."

"Nice-and New York is great," I chirp positively.

"Yeah, she loves it," she nods at me, then places her eyes back between the crosshairs.

"So do *you* go to school?"

"I did," she lowers the gun and relaxes her stance," two years of general studies at Rhode Island College before I realized... *I don't know* what I want to do."

"What do you like?"

"Adventure," she points the gun back up with intent on the target, "excitement."

"Well then, you're welcome," I smirk.

She smiles and points the gun at me, she fires two rounds.

"So what else do you do? Now that I know you're a martial artist, a dead eye, a sport climber, and a sassy pain in my ass. I'm intrigued, tell me more.

"Oh wow, you're intrigued? This is *so* exciting," she really lays into that sarcasm, "let's see, I love running, especially in warm rain, swimming, boats, big dogs, playing video games, watching horror and action films, I prefer tea over coffee, and my favorite color is purple. Your turn."

She picks a new target and fires.

"Uh, let's see – green, black coffee with maple syrup in it – don't judge me, video games, yes – I'm actually a huge pussy when it comes to horror movies," I stop talking to relish her smile and giggle. "I read a lot"

"*Really?*" she sounds shocked.

I take my sight off her target and place it on her instead.

"What's that supposed to mean?" I laugh once and drop my jaw mustering up the best look of disgust I can manage.

"No, you just... caught me by surprise is all." she checks me in the corner of her eye and smirks before firing at her target.

I quickly raise my gun and fire at her as I start to approach where she stands.

"I'm sorry!" She laughs playfully and she immediately begins backing away.

I ignore her apology and pick up speed. She shoots me and breaks into a run, wildly amused. Drugs don't affect me the way they do other people, but her laughter is like a drug that I can actually feel, and I can't get enough of it.

Damn she's fast. I drop my gun and demand more from my legs.

As soon as I'm nipping at her heals, I jump and twist catching her by the waist and shielding her from the impact that the ground brings with my body. She loses her gun. We skid to a stop and I roll over so that she's trapped beneath me. I hover myself above her, supporting my weight on my feet at either side of her torso, the only contact between us being where I have her wrists pinned above her head with my hands. She's still laughing up at me, enjoying the game as much as I am. I smile down at her like a geek. "What are you gonna do now?"

She composes herself with a long sigh and smiles devilishly.

"This."

I'm hit with a strong blow to the back. Her knees. I fall forward and in a matter of milliseconds, she's sitting on my back, planting my face into the floor. I turn my face to the side so I can spit out the leaves I ate in the landing.

"You got me," I smile "but – "

I push full force, flipping her off me. By the time I lock my sight on her, she has crawled away some. I grab her ankle and drag her back quickly trapping her beneath me again, this time pinning her legs with my ankles as I place my hands on both sides of her head.

"Could still use some work." I mock, rolling my eyes like I'm *speaking in all honesty.*

She narrows her eyes. I gaze down at her; her hair fanning out in the leaves, that smug determination – as usual – pitted in those dark eyes. Suddenly it feels as if there is a magnetic force reeling me in, I have no desire to fight it. I lower my face to hers, but as I close my eyes, I feel the barrel of her paintball gun press up into my chin. My eyes open to see her victorious expression, as I slowly force myself to back off.

"How 'bout lunch?" I sigh.

"Lunch," she repeats cheerfully with a nod.

I roll off of her and get to my feet before reaching back to help her up. She takes my hand and allows me to lift her up..

20.

Oops

We walk outside and spot the car where we left it. I circle back around Kael and pull the phone out of his back pocket. He turns and gives me a questioning look.

"I gotta call my dad. I have to let him know I'm alright."

I have to handle this. I feel like I can do it now.

He nods.

"Give me the keys. I'm gonna sit in the car."

He brushes the tip of his nose with his index finger and reaches into his pocket with his other hand retrieving the keys. He tosses them to me.

"Thanks. Wait here, OK? Just gimme a minute."

He nods again.

I walk around the car and hit the unlock button. I get in the passenger side and close the door. I watch Kael walk up to the back of the car and lean against the bumper. He remains facing the building. I look down at the phone in my hand.

What am I going to say to him? Do I lie? I can say I'm in New York with Frida. Say she had a bad break up or something and she needs me. It's the weekend, I've gone down to New York for the weekend. I gave him a heads up last time I did it though...

The phone starts vibrating in my hand. I look at the screen. 'HEAD.' Head? As in the people that are after me? They're calling Kael? I open the car door.

"Kael?"

"Yeah?" He answers over his shoulder without looking.

Would he have answered if he had the phone? Would he have told me? Why are they calling him?

"Never mind, ah... never mind."

I close the door and glance down at the phone right as it stops ringing. Time to do a little investigating. I hit redial and place the phone to my ear. It rings only once.

"Kael! Oh, *thank you*! *Thank you*! Listen to me. You need to bring her in. She's not safe out there," a man pleads on the other end

"This is Sophie Fileux."

There's a long pause.

"Sophie?"

"Yes."

"Where's Kael? Are you alone?" He seems very concerned by this possibility.

"No, he's outside."

"Outside where, where are you?"

"I'm sitting in a car, never mind that. What do you want with me? I know *what* I am, I just don't know what this *variation* is, and why Gage is dead because of it."

"Dead? They said Gage is dead? No. He's not dead. He's just... indisposed at this time."

"He's not dead?"

"Sophie, you're really not safe out there. You need to tell me where you are. I will send someone to get you."

"It won't work. Kael is too remarkably trained. I'll come to you, give me an address."

"No, absolutely not, I don't want you to go anywhere by yourself. Just let me talk to Kael, I can talk some sense into him. I can get him to listen."

"Kael lied to me. He said Gage was dead. That means I'm just leverage to get his brother back."

"Oh... that won't work."

"What do you mean it won't work?"

"Because, Gage… Gage can *not* be released at this time."

"Why not?"

"During one of our scheduled experiments... something... did not go as we expected. To be completely honest, we didn't know we were risking anything when we – " He pauses, clearly weighing how what he's about to say will affect my cooperation. "Long story short, the Gage who went into that operation room is not the Gage who came out. Quite frankly, he's a monster – but we're working on it! And you must know, this *will not* happen to you. I give you my word. We know better now. We're not even going to *run any tests* on you until we've exhausted all other options."

"You mean Gage? Exhausted *Gage?* Why should I trust you?"

"We're going to fix him. He *will* be the old Gage again. We have all the pieces of who he used to be. We just have to... find a way to put him back together. And all I'm asking you to trust right now is that we will keep you *alive*. I will explain everything, Sophie. We just need to get you to safety."

"Well Kael is not going to like that answer, so give me an address and I will get myself there. I can handle it fine. Just tell me where you want me to go and I will get there."

There's an exasperated sigh of defeat on the other line.

"Fine, just… go back to your house. I'll send a team out there. I really don't like this, Sophie."

"Well that makes two of us. When I see you I want some goddamn *answers*. You got me?"

"Understood. Be careful out there. Keep that phone on you from now until you are *standing in my presence*, if anything goes wrong, you call. Immediately."

"Whatever you say, chief." I click off the phone, dump it into the center console, jump over into the driver's seat, put the key in the ignition forcefully, and twist. The engine roars to life and I quickly throw the car into drive. I don't even look back to see Kael's reaction. I don't care. I can't believe this! I let him get in my head! I *trusted* him! He was just *using me*! Why didn't I see it earlier? I'm so stupid! My eyes start to fill with tears. No! I can't! Pull it together. Come on. I blink hard a couple times then glare at the road in front of me.

"What are you gonna do now, Kael, you stupid fuck! Huh? What's you next *bright* idea? Asshole!"

I pick up the phone, then press and hold the button until it beeps to signal that it's listening.

"How do I get to 15 Arrowhead Road, Glocester, Rhode Island, from here?"

"Let me check on that," the disembodied voice responds.

"You check on that," I snap like a crazy person.

"Starting route. To. Fifteen. Arrowhead. Road. Glocester. Turn right. Onto. Next exit."

This is gonna be a long drive.

21.

Final Preparations

I am on my way to turn myself in to the people I've spent the last two days hiding from. Am I insane, or is this actually the right choice? Am I doing this out of spite? To get back at Kael? A tear escapes the corner of my eye and trails down the side of my face before I quickly brush the dampness away with my forearm. It's a little to do with spite... but I'm not safe. I know that's true, and I'm not about to put my faith in Kael, that lying son of a bitch. He's not looking out for my well-being. It seems like either way I'm going to end up where I'm headed now. Shit! My house! Is Dad home? Fuck! What am I going to tell him! Hey Dad, how was work? Oh there's a team of secret agents coming to pick me up because I'm a science experiment. I should call him... maybe he doesn't think I'm missing. Maybe he didn't try calling me. Maybe he thinks we just keep missing each other. Bruce isn't home... he's not there to notice. Sometimes I don't see dad for days 'cause he's busy with work. We usually communicate by phone when that happens though... there is no chance he hasn't noticed... better call him. I dial the phone and he picks up on the second ring, which means it was probably the first ring for him.

"Who's this?"

"Dad, it' me – "

"Oh, hey baby. I'm sorry I haven't been home. Have you tried calling? I'm really into something over here. Who's phone you on?"

Oh my god, it's a miracle, and furthermore, it doesn't sound like he'll be making it home tonight either. In that case I need to set up a long term excuse for my extended absence.

"Oh, a new friend of mine." Saying that was harder on my emotional state than I had anticipated. I hold the phone as far away as my arm will allow and hold my breath until I feel like I've got a handle on myself. OK, OK, I'm good. I bring it back to my ear. "Hey, I just called to tell you that I'm not gonna be home for a little while. I'm goin' up to New York to stay with Frida."

"How long is a little while?"

"Like a week. Um, I called work and took some time. Kind of feel like I need to get away."

This way, I can call him in a week and say I got a bartending job on a whim, I've expressed interest in bartending before. Good money in tips. Then again, what if he tries to visit… too much to worry about right now, I'll have to work on this later.

"Well… OK, but be careful."

"'Kay, I will, love you Dad."

"Love you too. Keep in touch alright?"

"Yup, I'll talk to you later."

I hang up and toss the phone into the center again. Wonder what he's working on? Must be something big if he hasn't been home *and* hasn't called. Oh well, this works out great. Now I have to call Max. He might take a little more convincing. I dial the number. It rings once. Twice. Three times. Is he going to answer?

"Yeah"

He sounds like he just woke up.

"Max."

"Hey. What's up, kiddo, you alright?"

"Hi, Max. Yeah. I'm fine. Uh, listen. I need a week."

"You need a what now?"

Here we go.

"I'm going to New York."

"Are you kidding me?"

"No, I – "

"No, no. it's fine, it's Fine. You're right. Go, go. Go, go, go. It'll be good for ya. But if I find out you and your friend are doing any kind of drugs on that face-gram garbage, I will come down there and break that party up. You feel me?"

"No drugs. Cross my heart, Max."

"My eyes. Glued. To the phone, Soph. As of now."

"You realize I am not *required* to post everything I'm doing, right?"

"I'll find out. Don't do nothin' stupid, kid."

"*Alright* Max. I got it. I'll talk to you in a week."

"Yeah alright."

"Bye, Max."

"Yep."

I pull the phone away from my ear and click it off again. I press the corner of the cellular device onto my lips. What if I never see them again? I don't want to do this if they're not going to let me go. What am I doing? I don't know! I don't know what I'm doing! I don't know what they're doing! I don't know what they want me for! No. Don't think like that. Right now, all I know is that I am not safe out here. Priority one is staying alive. Just worry about that. Wait! My house looks like it's been broken

149

into! The door is gone! Dad's going to find out something's off when he gets there and it looks like that. Now I have to call that *head* guy back. I press the button on the top of the phone and alternate my attention between the road and the phone as I go into recents, find the number and tap it. It rings twice.

"Sophie. Talk to me. What's happening?"

"I'm on my way. But listen, I don't want my dad to find any of this out, so you have to do something about my house. Your guys broke the door down and there's dead – ."

"Oh, Sophie, we're professionals. That's already been taken care of. New door, unplugged the cooker. Food's in the fridge. There's nothing that will give your father any concerns."

"Oh... really?"

"It looks exactly like it did. Pre-forced entry."

"Oh... uh, thank you." I hang up the phone.

I put the phone in the center once more, placing it carefully this time face up. Everything is in order, just breathe.

Who knew this is where my life was going. Two days ago, I had normal problems like my piece of shit car, whether or not I'd give the guy from the climbing gym a shot, getting to work on time, figuring out what's for dinner. Now look, I mean what the actual fuck?

22.

Not a Chance

It's getting dark now. I turn onto my street. Here we go. Just breath. It's gonna be fine. Just stay calm, there's no turning back now. Everything is in order and there's nowhere else for me to go, I've committed to this decision. No turning back. I can see my house, the lights are on inside and there's a pair of black trucks in the driveway.

They're waiting for me inside. I just have to walk in that door and let them take me away. Just breathe, it's all alright. I've agreed to this, I'm not going anywhere against my will, they're going to protect me. Voluntary protective custody, that's all this is. I pull over to the side of the road before I reach my front yard.

OK, I've got this. I put the car in park and pick up Kael's cell phone. I stare at it for a moment.

He was gonna use me as leverage... I didn't even see it coming. I leave the keys in the ignition and get out of the car. Someone's going to need to drive this out of here. I turn and start making my way across the yard to the front door. I wonder what they're doing in there. Just waiting? Are they going to let me grab some things? I'm halfway there. The thunderous sound of a modified motorcycle engine fills the air. I know they do that so that other vehicles on the road know that they're there, but God is it obnoxious. I look up the street at the bike barreling down the pavement. All of the sudden it slows and I realize... shit! It's Kael! How the hell did he know I'd be coming here? He comes up onto the grass, lets the bike fall to the ground, steps over it, and starts making his way over to me in one motion. I turn back toward the front door and pick up the pace.

"Sophie!"

"You stay away from me!"

"Would you just stop and talk to me?"

I look at him over my shoulder while I continue walking.

"I don't want to talk to you!"

"Hey!" He catches up to me, grabs my arm and roughly turns me around. "Don't walk away from me! Do you have any idea? What if I didn't get here in time!"

"It would have made things a lot easier for me."

I turn around and try to yank my arm away from him, but he tightens his grip and turns me back around.

"Get in the fucking car Sophie! I can't believe – !"

"No." I grit my teeth.

"Excuse me?" He stares at me wide-eyed and his mouth is slightly agape.

"No! Get away from me!" I shout, hoping someone inside will hear me.

"Get your ass in that car or I will *put* you in that car."

"Let me go, Kael!"

"No," he says evenly.

"Let go of me!" I shout louder.

"Our world is not a world of rights and fairness and sugar plum fairies, Soph! If you go in there, you're dead, why don't you get that?"

"Because I *don't know* that!" I flail my free arm for emphasis

"Well luckily, until you can get through me, that doesn't matter much. Does it?" He barks coldly.

"Don't – "

Before I can finish my sentence Kael bends down grabs me by the back of my knees and lifts me up. I fall over his shoulder.

"No, Kael! Stop! Put me down! You can't do this!" I pound on his back with tight fists.

"I can. And I am."

"Kael, put me down!"

He ignores me and quickly strides to the car. He opens the door to the back seat behind the driver and tosses me in. Quickly I compose myself and jump halfway through the space between the front seats to lock the door before he can open it. I am successful. I actually wasn't expecting that would work. I must have caught him by surprise.

"Open the door, Soph!"

I jump over the rest of the way into the driver's seat and turn the key that I left in the ignition smiling triumphantly. I sense how Kael immediately understands my intent.

"Sophie, open the door!" He demands with more urgency.

I place my foot on the brake and put the car into drive.

"Hey, no, no, no, no, hey! Stop!"

I release the brake slowly but Kael runs around to the front of the car.

"Sophie! Don't do this!"

I keep creeping forward slowly.

"Stop!" He shouts banging both fists on the hood.

"Get out of the way, Kael!"

"No!"

"Move!"

"I'm *not* gonna move!"

I throw the car into reverse and slam on the gas, then switch it back into drive and swerve around him. He's too slow to jump back in front of the car and falls into the side of the vehicle as I pass him.

I drive up on the lawn to the front porch, jump out of the car and run to the door. I hear Kael hit the roof of the car and then he's behind me. How did he get here so fast? He wraps one hand around the bottom half of my face effectively covering my mouth, and the other arm around my waist.

I try to shout but can't get much noise through his grasp. He backs us up, away from the door. My feet leave the ground as I flail everything that I'm able to. I try to pull his hand away from my face with both of mine. Finally, he removes his hand from my mouth to open the back door of the car again.

"Kael!" I protest.

He tosses me back in the car and is in the driver's seat in record time with the door closed. I scramble for the door but he locks it before my hand reaches the handle.

"Let me out right now!"

Kael says nothing, he just drives.

I look out the window and see a group of armed men emerging from the house. *A lot of good they did.*

"That was too close," He utters mostly to himself.

"Stop the fucking car!"

"Jesus Christ! What the hell, Soph?"

"Just stop, Kael! Stop acting like you care! I trusted you! You're such a fucking asshole! Stop the goddamn car!"

"What the fuck are you tal – ?"

"I figured it out! Some guy from head called your phone! Gage is alive, and I know you know! This whole time I've just been your leverage!"

Kael whips the car around a corner and down a side road. Without saying a word, he pulls over, gets out of the car and slams the door shut. I watch him as he walks up to my door and yanks it open. He stares in at me matching my glare with one of his own.

"You never *were*, and you never *will* be leverage, Sophie."

"Is that so?" I spew facetiously.

"Listen to me!"

"Save it!"

"Luca called me. He told me Gage is alive. He was going to trade you in. That's why I changed my mind about Nebraska. We were going to Nebraska to meet up with Luca."

"Why should I believe that?"

"Because you are the best thing that's ever happened to me! Why would I give that up?"

I just stare up at him. Does he really mean that? It's hard to cling to my skepticism when I'm staring into those uncharacteristically sincere eyes. Those beautiful eyes. Stop it, Sophie! Don't! He's lying to you! He's been lying to you this whole time! You just want it to be true because... you... Ugh! You idiot! You've fallen for him, haven't you? You *like* him. Stupid! Stupid! Stupid!

I look away so I can review the facts without his distractingly perfect features.

"Sophie – "

"I can't!"

"You can't what?"

"Have *feelings* for you! I can't! I don't – that's not me! I don't know how to do that!"

"I don't know how either," he shrugs.

I hide my face from him.

"I can't change how I am. This is me. This is how I am."

"Sophie."

I look up, back into his eyes. He's leaning into the car suspending from the door and the hood by his hands.

"I don't *want* you to change."

I feel the goofy smile stretch across my face before I can stop it. He leans in closer.

"That was so cheesy," I giggle.

"I know, right? That was *actually* a little embarrassing."

His exaggerated grimace makes me laugh.

I lean forward and catch his mouth with mine. His left hand comes in and grips the back of my neck at the base of my skull holding me in place as he deepens the kiss. He gives a quick groan to signal that he has something to say and quickly pulls away, but not very far.

"Don't ever take off on me like that again. Please."

"Well then don't withhold information. It looks suspicious."

"I didn't want to freak you out. I couldn't tell you my plan was ruined and I had no idea what I was going to do."

"You *could* have, and next time you *will*."

"We'll see." He retreats from the car. "Get in the front, we gotta go."

Sighing, I get out and walk around the back of the car to get to the other side. Kael closes the back door and sits back in the driver's seat. I open the passenger door and hear the squealing of tires. My eyes shoot up to the street corner we turned down to find one of the black trucks from the driveway. Then another.

"Sophie, get in!"

I jump into the seat, pull the door closed and the engine roars. We shoot forward. I look behind at the trucks gaining on us.

"Kael, I don't think we should run."

"What are you talking about?" Kael shouts, taking a short cut over someone's front yard.

"I talked to that guy. He said I'm not safe. That's why they're after me. They want to protect me."

"Yeah? And who's going to protect you from them? Oh wait! Me!"

"Kael, something is obviously going on here. You don't even know why they need me. I can't spend my whole life avoiding this. Sooner or later, I'm going to have to go through it. Might as well be now. Think about it. If I have cooperation on my side, I'll be able to make sure they grant you immunity. We don't have to *disappear,* we just have to *cooperate.* That's how we get our lives back."

"Is that what this is about? You think things can just go back? They're not going to let you go! They told us Gage was dead because they don't plan on *releasing* him. That's what they meant. He's dead to *us.* They didn't want us asking about him anymore. This is what they do."

Shit. That sounds like... there might be some truth to that...

I look back at the trucks behind us again.

"Can't this thing go any faster?" I complain.

"Those trucks are pretty fast themselves."

"Clearly."

The truck bumps us, sending us forward in our seats but Kael doesn't let up on the gas.

"Son of a bitch!" He turns and glares at the back window. "You can't fucking have her!"

I see another black truck on the other side of the road up ahead driving toward us. It abruptly switches into our lane.

"Kael! Road!"

He turns just in time to swerve out of the way of the oncoming truck. Unfortunately, the swerve cost us our upright position on the street.

I've never been in a car accident before. I watch the road meet the windshield once. Then on the second roll I see grass. By the time I see grass the second time the top of the car is much closer. And...

23.

Answers

"Sophie?"

Mmm, go away!

"Sophie?"

"Yeah, what?" I mutter without opening my eyes.

"Sophie, I'm Dr. Myles DeWitt. We spoke on the phone."

My eyes fly open and I seek out the owner of the voice I've been hearing calling my name on and off for what – now that I have my wits about me – must have been around fifteen minutes.

"Where's Kael?"

"Agent Hues is fine. He's in the room next door."

"I want to see him."

"I'm afraid that's not possible right now."

"Why not? Is he OK?" I demand anxiously. We were in an accident! What if he got hurt?

"Because the room next door is a holding cell. But I assure you he's fine."

"Why is he in a cell?"

"Because he's a threat," he answers, clearly assuming as much should be obvious.

"He was just trying to protect me! He's not a threat!"

"That's apparently exactly why he *is* a threat. He doesn't seem to trust us very much right now and until we're all on the same page, the cell is where he must stay. It's for your safety, you understand."

"No I don't understand. I don't. Because if you are worth trusting, it shouldn't be very hard to get him on the same page. Tell him the truth. Tell him what he needs to know. Show him his brother. That's what this all comes down to. And while you're at it, tell him *and me* – seeing as it's the same reason you need me – why you took his brother in the first place. What is this *variation*?"

He breaks eye contact for the first time looking down and to the right. Dad would say that this indicates internal dialog. He is weighing the pros and cons of what he's going to share and whether or not he *will* in fact share. This guy is easy to read, Kael doesn't have any tells... as far as I can tell... so far. I'll have to remember to pay closer attention to him from now on. But the eye thing was really drilled into me so, force of habit I guess.

"OK, you win. This will help you to understand why we are so desperate to keep you here. Alive. Available to us – "

"If it'll help me understand why would you withhold it in the first place. The easiest way to get someone on your side is to tell them exactly why you're on their side! Why does no one know this?"

"Because it's a lot to take in – "

"Yup, I've heard that one before, too. I can handle it! Come on, lay it on me. The amount of shit I've dealt with in the past two days, because everyone trying to spare my fragile little mental state, is astounding, and above all – insulting."

"Sophie, we may have found a way to make spontaneous regeneration possible, and you and Gage are the only key we have to it."

"Spontaneous – ?"

"Spontaneous regeneration."

"Meaning?"

"The nearly immediate regeneration of damaged, degraded cellular tissue – including on an osteo level – not only healing the most fatal wounds at a remarkable rate but also maintaining cellular health to its highest capacity. Do you know what that means?"

"I can get shot and not die of the gunshot wound?"

"Even more than that, it means you won't die, period. You will not age. And you cannot be killed. Immortality."

Immortality? What? How is that – it's impossible.

"No," I state simply. "No, that's impossible."

"No. Sophie *you* are impossible, a synthetic human being. You and Gage and Kael... yet here you all are. We are at the brink of what will change the world – the future, forever. And *you* put us on that brink, you and Gage. If we lose you, that future gets infinitely less attainable. Humanity may never get another shot at this. We can't take any unnecessary risks."

"I see. Just... give me a minute, OK? Can you just – "

I pull my knees up to my chest and drop my head between them.

"Do you need some water?"

"Nope. No I just need you to get out," I stipulate matter-of-factly.

"Oh, right, yes, OK... well I'll – "

"Yup, out." I nod my head yes.

"Kay, I'll be back later."

24.

The Subject

I stay balled up on the bed, head between my legs, for what feels like hours and all I can keep thinking is... immortality... this isn't real. Someone is seriously fucking with me because this shit does not happen. This is real life, people can't live forever and perform hits at eight years-old, and make people with computers and machines and test tubes... well test tubes, yes, there's a such thing as test tube babies but the stuff *in* the test tube came from a human male... a normal human male, nothing was done to it in transport. Or maybe there was... maybe I'm not number ten. Maybe I'm number a million and fucking – I don't know – 73 and they've been messing with all the test tube babies since they *started* making test tube babies.

A knock rips me from my inner rants. I fling my head up to glare at the closed door. I can't help but notice the room for the first time as I do this. White, medical, and professional looking, in other words boring – *painfully* boring.

"If you're not Kael, I don't want to talk to you."

Another couple of knocks pass through the metal door. I get up, cross the room, and turn the handle. I swing the door open. Kael stands there grinning at me.

"Kael! What the hell? How – ?"

Before I realize what I'm doing, I jump at him, wrapping my arms around his neck and resting my head on his shoulder. Of course he catches me, wrapping his own arms around my waist.

"Miss me?"

"Oh my god, I was going crazy!" I trill, letting go of his neck and sliding down to my feet. He doesn't let go of me, which strangely for me, I don't mind.

"I'll bet I can guess why." His tone has changed slightly and I immediately know that he knows.

I look down and rest my forehead on his chest. His arms raise up to the middle of my back and pulls me tightly against him. I turn my head and press my cheek to his chest so that I can continue to breathe.

"This is huge," I sigh.

"I can see how *some* would think so."

"Some?"

"*The point is*, you are still *you*. Don't forget that. Immortality is not something the world *needs,* it's something that these guys think will *improve* it."

Hmm, he's not terrible at changing the angle. That does make me feel a little better.

"Thanks – "

"But," he interrupts. "This *does* mean that you are not safe... out there... until all of the activists have been taken out, their evidence destroyed, and no one remains to pick up where they left off."

I pick up my head and back away to look him in the face.

"Well… if they make it so I can't die – "

"No." Another familiar voice interrupts. "We're not even going to consider trying anything with you until we don't have any other choice. I assured you of that myself."

It's the man from earlier, *Dr. Something DeWitt.* I push Kael's hands away to face the approaching lab coated man coming down the hall.

"So… how long are we talking here?

He reaches us and stops walking.

Both of them are awkwardly silent.

"I can't stay here for the rest of my life!"

"Sophie – " Kael starts with an apologetic tone.

"No!" I shout.

Kael turns to DeWitt.

"Why don't you give us some space. I'll talk to her."

"Kael, no!" I object.

DeWitt narrows his eyes at Kael but then starts to walk away, continuing down the hallway. "I'll be back with food later."

"No! Wait!" I start to follow him but Kael catches my arm. "Come back here! We have to talk about this – "

"Sophie." Kael interrupts.

"No, Kael! I'm not staying here!"

"Calm down Soph. It's just *for now*."

I watch the doc walk down the hall and turn a corner. I turn around and look at Kael.

"It's just for now." He repeats.

"Why are you playing nice?"

Kael grabs hold of my hips and backs me into the room.

"Because it's the only way they'll let me *stay with you*." He says urgently in a hushed tone.

He removes one of his hands and closes the door. Then his hand returns to my hip and his thumb finds its way under my shirt skating back and forth across my skin to the extent of its reach before hooking into the waist of my jeans.

"Are you trying to change the subject, Agent Hues? If I didn't know any better, I'd say you're trying to distract me. I don't much appreciate that," I smile playfully.

"Oh? Well maybe you'll appreciate *this*."

His mouth is on mine and I can't hide my appreciation. I was worried about him. I'm glad they are letting me keep him at least.

I pull away and he is visibly disappointed.

"And they trust you?" I ask skeptically raising an eyebrow.

"To an extent. I've agreed to voluntary nighttime confinement. If I wanna stay, I've gotta sleep in the cell," he grimaces.

"How long is this going to be? Like can you give me a rough estimate?" I look around. "This place... do I have to stay *inside* the building?"

"Don't get hung up on details like that yet. What matters right now, tonight, is that it's safe."

I take a deep breath and let it out.

"Right. Safe. Cool." I agree half-heartedly, unsure myself whether or not I mean it.

"And I'll be here."

"As long as you behave," I add with a smirk.

He pulls me closer and tilts his face down so it's inches from mine.

"I can be very good," he narrows his eyes playfully.

"Can you? I think I'm going to need some convincing."

He starts backing me further into the room until I feel the bed pressing against the back of my legs.

"Convincing?" He scoffs, "can't you just trust me?"

"Mmm' nope," I smile.

The corners of his mouth twitch just before it meets mine and my eyes flutter closed. I wrap my arms around his neck. The hand under my shirt slides up from my hip to my lower back. His tongue slides gently across my lower lip, prompting invitation. I part my lips to gasp and he lets himself in. The feeling is wonderful. I'm lifted off my feet and released so that I fall back onto the mattress. Immediately Kael grabs hold of the bottoms of my jeans and yanks, sliding them off my legs before discarding them to the floor. Then he jumps on the bed on top of me, supporting his weight with his knees and forearms. I giggle.

"You look more comfortable without pants on."

"Do I?"

"Mmmhmm."

"Well then thank you for taking it upon yourself to remove them. You know I think you would be more comfortable without a shirt on."

"You think?"

"Mmm, so constricting." I smile up at him. "Let me help you with that."

I grab the bottom of his shirt and start to drag it up. He holds his arms up so that I can get it over his head.

"Oh wow, yeah, you're right," he quips. "You should try this."

I laugh and put my arms up above my head. The hands under my shirt drag up my back teasingly pulling the material along. He pushes the shirt over my face and up my arms. Once the shirt is gone, he keeps my arms there, holding them in place by my wrists as he lowers his face to mine again. He demands entrance immediately this time. His hands glide down my arms and over my sides caressing my hips at the edge of my underwear. He hooks his fingers underneath. His tongue swirls around my own making me moan. He parts my legs with one of his knees and gets between them. I push his chest away. He stops and looks at me.

"Do you have a condom?"

"Nah, I can pull out, it's fine."

"Like hell you can – get the fuck off." I push him.

171

"I was kidding!" he laughs. "Look, I'm way ahead of you," He holds up the small square package so I can see it. I stick my index finger in his face.

"That's not funny." I tell him sternly.

"Kinda funny," he winces his face in disagreement. He smacks my hand away and closes the distance between us. I break away to speak again.

"Not Fun – "

25.

Terms

A knock at the door wakes me from my sleep. It's dark in the room, but I can still see the outline of Kael passed out face down beside me. There's another knock. Shit!

"Kael," I whisper as loud as I can.

I try to get up but Kael's arm is pinning me down.

"Kael," I whisper again and shake him.

I try to push his arm up and slide out from underneath but he stirs and tightens his grip.

"What? what?" He asks frantically.

The knock sounds again, louder than before.

"Ah, fuck." He utters as he jumps up grabbing my pants and throwing them to me. I pull them on in time to catch my shirt with my face. I wrench it away to glare at Kael who's already dressed and smiling at me.

"Thanks" I mutter and pull on the shirt.

"Glad to help." he flashes his teeth and points at the pile of undergarments on the floor.

I push them under the bed with my foot and nod. Kael turns on the light and opens the door to find the good doctor holding a tray full of food.

"DeWitt," Kael chimes.

"Kael," he takes a noticeable observation of the situation in here, "I brought you guys some stuff to eat..." He looks down at what he's holding "Oatmeal, grapes, toast."

"Um, thanks." I take the tray.

"Alright." He brings his hands together and rubs them slowly. "So I'm actually off to D.C. for a presidential conference to report our new situation, but when I'm back here tomorrow, I'll show you around the building and we'll talk about any and all of your concerns. We know how difficult it's going to be for you to stay inside the facility, but it's for your protection. So as long as we're all on the same page and accept the terms, you'll have full range of the entire building. There are twelve floors to this place. Three below ground, nine above. This is only the bottom floor; you'll have plenty of room to stretch your legs. Furthermore, we'll let you make adjustments. Say you want a theater, it's yours. We've got the room and resources for anything you can think up."

"But how long is this for?"

"We'll talk about that tomorrow when I get back."

I drop my gaze in defeat for the time being.

"Lights out soon, alright?" He looks from me to Kael. "That means I need *you* in the cell."

He stares at Kael. I realize it has become a contest to see who will look away first. Finally, Kael looks at me, grabs two pieces of toast off the tray, and takes a bite out of both at once like it's an empty sandwich as he walks to the door to be lead away.

"See you in the morning, Soph," Kael sighs, his mouth still full of bread.

The two exit the room and walk down the hall. I look out to see what direction they're going in but they turn down a hallway and I can't see them anymore. I pull my head back in the room and close the door with my back. Oatmeal and grapes doesn't sound awful. I place the tray on the end table next to the bed and grab a couple grapes and the bowl of oatmeal.

Plopping my butt down on the bed, I pop the grapes in my mouth and grip the spoon in my hand. Oatmeal. This was the

175

last thing I ate in my house. I *will* leave this place. I *will* see my house again. This isn't forever. I'll see Bruce again, I'll see dad, and I'll see Frida... If only I really was in New York right now... I wonder if Frida will like Kael.

Kael... I *really* like him. I never thought this would be me. I thought I was going to die alone someday... turns out I might not die at all. No, I don't want to think about that right now, I'm feeling pretty good. I just had sex. I don't have to worry about being killed in my sleep tonight. Life is good for now... as long as I don't think too much about it.

I take a bite of my oatmeal and lift my shirt to look at the cut in my ab. It doesn't look awful but I should probably tell DeWitt about this tomorrow when he brings me breakfast. I wish Kael could have stayed in here. There's nothing to distract me now and I have to distract myself. Maybe I'm tired enough to fall back asleep. I am tired... I shovel in a few more bites as I stand up and pull the covers down on the bed. Then I get on my knees and pull my underwear out from under the bed. I place the bowl on the bed and shake out of my jeans. I leave them on the floor and pull on the panties. I pick the bowl back up and take another bite before placing it back on the tray. I skip over to the light switch and flick it off, then run back, slide into bed, and pull the covers up.

Please fall asleep. Please fall asleep...

26.

Greetings

A knock on the door wakes me again. Well, rather a banging this time. It makes me anxious... who's *banging*? What time is it? It's still dark. But then again, there are no windows so that doesn't really mean anything. Maybe I can get myself a room on one the floors above ground. I refuse to live like a mole person. If I'm gonna be in here long, I need sun.

The banging sounds again, equally as anxiety inducing.

Is this how it's always going to be? After these past couple days, is it too much to ask that I wake up on my own?

It could be morning I guess, but I don't *feel* like I've been sleeping that long. It *would* mean that I get Kael back soon, though. I wonder what time in the morning they're going to release him from the cell? Is it going to be the same time every morning or is it going to be informal... how long before they trust him enough to not put him in there anymore. Will that ever happen?

I get out of the covers and slide my feet to the floor.

"Coming. Hold on."

I pull my jeans on and walk to the door.

"Just a second"

I turn the light on and open the door.

The next thing I know I'm on the floor. A bat. I got hit in the head... with a bat. Ow! Fuck man! That fucking hurts! I hold my head and hope the aftershock will pass soon. How long have I been down here? Fuck it's like I'm still getting hit, I can't recoil from the pain! It's throbbing!

"People aren't meant to live forever!" Someone bellows.

The bat comes again. Into my side I ricochet into the wall and hug myself. I look up, but all I see is the bottom of someone's foot approaching the center of my vision alarmingly fast. I don't know how many more kicks to the head I can take. Then I feel the bat again. Maybe there's more than one...

"Stop!" I shout desperately in a voice I don't recognize.

I hold up my hands to block my face, I don't know where else to block because my eyes are screwed shut. But I know I have

178

to protect my head. I instinctively try to shrink myself into a ball, to make myself a smaller target. But it doesn't help. Blow after blow. I just wait for it to end... there's nothing more I can do.

Suddenly I hear a cry that didn't come from me. The feet and bats are gone but the pain remains. I try to open my eyes but it hurts too much. This doesn't make sense. What stopped them?

"Sophie?" A new voice asks in a curious yet apathetic tone. "Is that *you*?"

Finally, I open my eyes. It's fuzzy and bright at first. But then my eyes focus. Who's this guy? Rust colored hair and dull blue eyes. Head cocked to one side, unnervingly smug grin plastered on his face. Somehow the experience is equal to when I first saw Kael. Perfect features. Cold eyes. Only when it was Kael, his eyes softened. These are like stones.

"Who – ?"

"Gage," he answers quickly. "It's nice to finally meet you Miss Fileux."

What? Gage? As in *Gage* Gage? *Kael's* Gage?

"Now what do you say we go find my favorite sibling." He continues. His voice oozes with a sarcasm that would put Kael to shame.

He roughly grabs my upper arm and hoists me to my feet.

"Where are – ?"

I can't seem to finish my thought aloud or even in my head, but he immediately understands what I'm getting at.

"They're all dead. Big group of the dumb bastards broke in. Guess I *should* be thanking them though. Weren't for them trying to kill me, I never would'a got loose." He drags me out of the room and we start down the hall. "Everyone else that was here is dead too. I killed them all – all the ones I could find anyway – so things are *looking up*."

27.

Consequence

"**O**h big brother! Look what I've found."

"Gage?" Kael's confused voice echoes down the hall.

Where's this going? We continue until we round the corner. Kael is pressed up to the bars looking through at me and Gage. His eyes widen as he evaluates the situation.

"I am locked up in this prison. Tortured day in and day out. Because your main *concern* is your main *squeeze* here."

He grips the back of my neck and squeezes. I wince. My legs would give out if it weren't for his abrasive support.

"Gage! No! Don't you touch her!"

"Mmm, s'a little late for that, bro. I mean look at her. She's a little banged up already. Can't you see? Well, maybe you need a better view."

With that he throws me into the bench in front of the cage wall. I topple to the floor bringing the bench with me and slide to a stop in front of the bars just out of Kael's limited arm's reach.

"Sophie! I'm so sorry, Soph! I'm so sorry! I'm gonna get you outta this alright? I'm gonna… I'm gonna get you out! Just hold on, alright?" His voice is near my head but I can't turn my face up to see him.

I hear Gage's footsteps approaching me, then the bench is kicked out of the way.

"No! Leave her alone Gage! She's had enough! You're gonna kill her! What do you want? Huh? What do you want from me?"

"I *want you* to watch."

He kicks me in the side and I feel like I'm going to throw up. I ball up on the floor and hug my stomach.

"No! No! Stop! Gage stop! Don't!"

All I can hear is Kael's bellowing voice and banging metal. He kicks me again.

"Gage! Make *me* suffer not her! Take it out on *me*!"

"I plan to. Wanna see how?"

182

He kicks me again and I cry out and sob once into my hand before composing myself the best I can.

"You know, your girl is tough. *That* was the most noise she's made so far. Let's see what other kinds of noises we can get out of her, shall we?"

"Please! Gage, no! I am begging you," Kael half sobs.

"I did a lot of begging too, Kael. They didn't stop. But let me tell you, just because it didn't *kill me*, doesn't mean it didn't hurt like *fucking hell!* I *wished* I could die... do you know how that feels? To *wish* you could die? It puts some things into perspective, let me tell you."

"I'm sorry Gage! I didn't know what was going on here!"

"No. You're not. You're not sorry! You're not even listening to the words coming out of my mouth! You're just trying to take my attention off her! You left me in here! You let them *do* this to me!"

He bends down, grabs a fist full of my hair and lifts me from the ground. I grab the top of my head with both arms as he sets me up into a standing position.

"Just leave her out outta this! Let her go! This is between you and me!"

"Leave her out of this? Man, are you serious? This *whole thing*- is about her! It's between *me and her.* I'm just fuckin' *pissed* at *you. She's* the one that got to live while I was stuck in here. What happened to *ladies first*? It should have been *her* in here, not me. I fuckin' work for them, who's she? Huh? Why were they willing to risk *me* before *her*?" He stops and takes a breath to calm himself down. "So I'm gonna fill her in on everything she missed out on."

Gage lets go of my hair and catches me by the waist on my way back down to the floor. Then he grabs my arm with his free hand and wraps it around his neck and hoists me up so that I'm standing, supported by his weight. We start turning.

"What are you doing? Where are you taking her?" Kael demands.

"Exam room one... that's where *I* started."

"Gage!"

He starts walking me down the hall. My feet sweep over the floor like the useless things they've become.

"Gage! Get back here! Don't you touch her! Don't you fucking touch her!"

"See you later Kael. Sophie, say 'bye Kael."

"Kael?" I whimper pathetically.

"Sophie! Just hold on I'm gonna get you out of this! I promise! I'm coming for you, do you hear me? I'm coming to get you!"

"Don't make promises you can't keep," Gage calls back.

"Don't do this, Gage!"

Gage continues dragging me down the hall. Escorting me further from Kael's desperate pleas and deeper into hopelessness. We pass through a door and down another hallway where we arrive at an elevator and stop.

"You have *a lot* of catching up to do, Sophie."

"Why are you doing this?" I'm barely audible but the sentence still costs me all the air in my lungs.

"Because it's fair."

"It's not fair... it's not fair what they did... to you... but it's not my... fault..."

"It's not my fault either."

"You're the one who's... doing this."

"You don't get it."

"No... I guess... not." I wince. "Why don't you fill me in."

He punches the button to call the elevator with the side of his closed fist.

"Why don't *you* keep your attitude in check."

"Why? You're gonna kill me either way... might as well be myself, I don't have much... longer to do it."

"Kill you? I'm not gonna kill you," he laughs. "I'm gonna make you indestructible."

"Wha – ?"

"Over the months I was here, I had a lot of time to think this through. If I have to live forever... so do you."

"I don't understand?"

"I know you don't, so let me finish. You see, Sophie, I'm scared. No... I'm *terrified*. Because what is the one rule that is forever?"

I use everything in me to look up at him with narrowed eyes.

"Say please and thank you?" I grumble.

"That *nothing* is forever... *everything* ends. So what happens when the world is gone and I'm still here? Hmm? You get me?"

"So what's your plan... what's happening here?" I inquire with slightly more urgency.

"My plan is that Kael and DeWitt and all them are not going to rest until there's a way to undo this... for your sake. You are going to make them see my side of this, because it'll be *your* side too. And they'll listen, 'cause you're the special one. And if they fail... at least I won't be existing in the absence of everything we know by myself, I'll have *you* to talk to.

I stare up at him in horror. I never thought of what immortality would actually mean for me.

"We're in this together, you and me," he adds with a smirk.

186

"We would *never* be in it together, Gage."

"Sure we will."

"How do you figure?"

"Because eventually *you'll* need someone too, and all you'll have is me."

The doors to the elevator slide open and he pushes me inside. I fall into the back wall and grab hold so I won't end up on the floor. I need to do *something*.

"How will you be able to live with yourself having subjected someone to that?"

"Well, see, I thought of that and realized that morality would eventually fade and I'd be kicking myself from then on. So I decided plan B is a much better in the long run. You'd do the same thing." He steps in and turns to press a button.

I spot a semi-automatic handgun poking out the back of his pants.

"No I wouldn't," I retort keeping my eyes on the gun.

The doors close and we start to move. He turns his head and looks at me over his shoulder. I immediately look up as to not clue him in on my intentions.

"You're lying to yourself," he says simply.

He turns back around, facing the doors.

"What did they *do* to you?" I utter, disgusted with his coldness.

"Fun fact for future reference, once you're like me... you will be able to grow back limbs... any body part actually. Lungs, heart... things got a little screwy after they took a piece of my brain. If they got word that someone local needed an organ donor, they jumped on the opportunity to... the funny thing about this *thing*... this *spontaneous regeneration* bullshit... is that Novocain and sedatives don't do shit for more than two seconds before my body wears it off. So they had no choice but to proceed regardless. Hey, s'not like it's gonna kill me, right? The shock sometimes left me staring at the ceiling of my cell for days on end before I finally snapped out of it. I couldn't move, *nothing* was going through my head... it was...." He pauses and shakes his head as if trying to shake the memory away. "When I finally did come to, I would just yell my fucking head off... I couldn't... stop."

The image he painted in my head makes me shudder, which he sees in my reflection on the elevator doors before they open. He turns back to me and grabs me under my armpit and trudges forward keeping his eyes ahead of him. I wait for my foot to reach the edge of the elevator door before I grab the gun and yank back hard. Gage isn't expecting it and loses his grip on me. I slap the door button on the wall of the elevator in my descent to the floor firing the gun at Gage all the way down so that the doors can close without his interference until I hear the click,

click, click of an empty cartridge. The doors slide closed right before Gage can stick his hand in.

I stumble to my feet as quickly as I can manage. I've gotta get Kael out but I can't do it by myself. Not like this. I have to get out of this place. DeWitt said that there are twelve floors to this building.

The doors start to open.

"No!" I shout at them as I slap the 'close doors' button again and smash Gage's hand with the empty gun until it disappears and the doors close back up.

Three floors underground and nine levels above. I drop the gun and press the four button and start to move.

Exhaling a breath I was apparently holding, I lean my forehead on the wall above the buttons and watch them light up as I move up floors. It's hard to breathe, as if one of my broken ribs has actually pierced my lung. He won't go after Kael, he's coming after me. The elevator slows to a stop and the doors open. I poke my head out to check the coast. Clear. But I must say I'm disappointed. Couldn't this elevator just transport me to the front entrance? Is that really asking too much?

I carefully step out. Holding the wall for support, I start making my way down the hall. I've got to go faster than this, come on. Move Sophie. He's gonna catch up. I step away from the wall and break into a weak sprint. My head is buzzing and

189

I'm starting to feel nauseous. Why aren't there any windows! It's just doors as far as I can see. I need to get to the end and then I'll try the room wherever that is. The room on the end has to have a window, right? I'm gonna go with that for now. This hallway stretches on forever! I can't go any faster than this! This is never going to work!

This hallway seems so familiar for some reason... it brings my anxiety level up higher. I can see the last door at the end. It's still far away. I focus on it. My vision starts to do this pins and needles thing and my head feels weird. I have to stop for a second. Just a second. I lean into the wall and slide down to the floor. I bring my hands to my forehead and breathe. Where is Gage? It's really good that he hasn't caught up yet, but *why hasn't he* caught up? This is too good to be true. What's going on? It doesn't matter. Just get up. I have to get out. *And go where?* I don't know, I'll figure it out when I get there. Get to the road. Find out where I am. Find someone with a phone. *Come on move it.* Alright, OK. Go.

I lift myself from the floor and head for that last door. Don't even look back, you're almost there. Come on. It's getting closer. Just like 100 more feet, 100 more feet that's nothing. That's nothing, Sophie, you're a *runner*! So *run*! Come on. My feet awkwardly slap the floor under me. Almost there.

I fall into the closed door and grab the handle for support. Turn, turn, turn! Oh! Thank god it's not locked. That would have been *it*. I stumble into the room and close the door behind me. I look, no lock on the door. Damn. Quickly I survey the room. White brick walls. Windows, relatively high up, but with a large ledge that I can climb up on. I cross the distance and scale the wall with moderate difficulty. Ugh, man I hurt so bad. I'm not used to aches like this. I've never met anything but ease pulling stunts like this. I look out the window, there's a wide patch of grass outside hugging the building before it turns to a tar parking lot, I see the white lines marking parking spaces. I look for a way to open the window but it's no use. These don't open, I'll have to smash it. I line up my elbow and face the door I entered through on the other side of the room. One. Two. Three. My arm crashes through. I feel the outside breeze, it feels wonderful. But I see the door opening.

I instantly lose interest in attempting to land gracefully on my feet. Without even turning around, I push myself out the window, and brace myself for the ground.

28.

The Passing

And it comes… the wind is ripped from my chest. My body goes numb… suddenly it feels like I'm struggling to keep my eyes open. I feel so tired… but it makes no sense, I wasn't this tired a second ago… I was weak, but this is something different. The numbness fades a little and I feel really cold. It's extremely uncomfortable… I wish the cold would go away… it's summer, why do I feel like I'm lying in a tub of ice cubes? What is that taste? What's in my mouth… ugh, there's so much of it, it's runny. I turn my head and spit. It's thick, glossy and black in the grass. I wipe my mouth with the back of my right hand to examine it. It's not black it's red, in its richest hue. *Aw no.*

Forget about it, *Concentrate*! Get up! He's coming! You have to get up! I put my hand down but I can't... get myself to move. My body isn't working for some reason.

Without consulting my brain, I clench my stomach muscles, attempting, unsuccessfully, to sit up.

I can't make sense of why I'm screaming, but I can't stop either. Why can't I stop? When the shrieking finally subsides, I placed my hands back on the ground and shift my body, trying to flip over onto my stomach. Maybe if I get up a different way... I stop when I start screaming again. What the hell? This is beginning to aggravate me; why do I keep screaming? Suddenly I can't hear the sound of my scream anymore, but the tickling vibration on my eardrums ensures that it's not because I stopped. I try to pinpoint the origin of this agonizing pain I'm apparently feeling.

I notice my right hand is wrapped around something sharp and resting on my left shoulder. I don't remember moving my hand there, and I certainly don't remember picking up a piece of broken glass before I did. My hand must have been squeezing the window shard pretty hard, because it and my hand are completely stained with deep red. I go to bring the shard closer to my face to inspect it further. My hand doesn't move. Why isn't it moving? I tug on it again, harder this time, causing a wave of agony to come crashing down on me. I *feel* the pain

193

this time, so I don't mind allowing the inevitable shriek rip through my chest.

The bubble of mental numbness I was in a minute ago is gone now and in its place is excruciating pain. I stare at the glass in my hand and slowly begin to unravel my fingers one at a time. I pull the last finger away, and the five-inch-tall, three-inch-wide shard remains balanced on my shoulder under my collar bone.

No! No! No! This is not good! Please, no! I close my eyes and pray for loss of consciousness.

I fell on my back! The glass is not just jutting out the front of me! It's sticking in *through my back*! The other side of the glass is probably stuck in the dirt, and that's why when I tried to sit up before I didn't go anywhere. I try moving my left arm and immediately declare it immobile when the searing pain intensifies

Alright, come on. Suck it up Sophie. This doesn't change anything! He's still after me, I have to move! He's got Kael in there, I have to get help! Just move, do it now! The numbness is gone, so at least I'm coherent. The pain woke me up a bit, and I don't feel like I'm on the brink of a coma anymore. I clench my stomach muscles again since that seemed to cause the least amount of pain within my two attempts to get off the ground. I cry out savagely, but don't stop until I pull the glass out of the ground behind me and I'm in a sitting position with my right arm placed behind my back for support. Ah! No *good, no* good!

I look around until I see Gage leaning against the wall of the building not far from me. He's looking at a syringe that he's got in his hand filled to capacity with a red liquid. He holds it up above eye level and taps it twice with his middle finger, then pulls an elastic tourniquet off his bicep with his needle wielding hand.

"That was some move you pulled," Gage complements sarcastically without removing his eyes from the syringe. "Good job." He shakes his unoccupied thumb at me as he turns the needle into position in his other.

No. Not that.

"To bad about the glass though." He motions to the object of my impalement. "I was looking forward to seeing what you'd do to yourself next."

I push off the ground with my feet and left arm, then twist my waist around until I can throw my left leg over my right and land on my knees. Then with my right arm, I grab the ground in front of me, carefully placing my left foot to avoid the glass, and rise up keeping my hand on the ground until my right foot is stabilized. It wasn't until now, while I'm standing on it, that I realize another pain in my left leg. I look down and see another shard of glass sticking about three inches out the back of my calf. It looks a little wider than the shard in my shoulder. I reach down, grit my teeth and pull it out as fast as I can which isn't very. It frees from my leg. I probably should have left it alone. Now it's gushing blood...

"Oof, that was gross," Gage groans. You're stronger than I gave you credit for... I thought you were going to stay down, but look at you go."

I ignore him, and start limping away.

"How long are you going to keep this up?" Gage asks following a few feet behind me.

I cringe with every step, taking wider strides whenever I can manage.

"I know I said I wanted to see what you would do, but... you don't look so good... you're losing an awful lot of blood..."

I just keep moving... and he keeps following.

The world around me starts spinning. I close my eyes to fight the dizziness that the swirling colors are causing. When I open them, the spinning has stopped, but I'm back on the ground lying on my unimpaled side with my right arm outstretched in front of me. I feel the numbness slowly start creeping back over me. Frantically, I begin grabbing the ground ahead and pulling it toward me with all that's left of my strength while cautiously staying off my left side. DeWitt's gotta be on his way right? I just gotta drag this out as long as I can... and make sure he can fix me without giving me that *stuff*. I don't want it. I don't want to live forever with this fucking monster!

"Come on now, Sophie. This is getting sad. Where exactly do you think you're going?" He chuckles. "There's no running from this, it's happening."

I can't... feel anymore... am I still moving? Why aren't my eyes open? Opening them is a difficult task but when I can finally see out of them I look back and see Gage getting closer. And that's it...

I hear a thud.

"Soph?" I hear... Kael?

"Fucking shit! Hey!" His voice grows louder. I'm moved around a bit, I'm not face planted on the black top anymore, I'm flipped over but my back isn't on the ground.

"Hey!" I feel his palm pat my cheek three times. "Hey! Open 'em up!" His fingers pry one of my eyelids open and I focus on his face.

"Oh hey." I feel my lips spread and curl at the corners. "Am I... glad to see you. You're never gonna believe this one."

"We gotta get you inside. There's gotta be something in there that can help us." he rambles desperately.

"I fell out a window," I chuckle weakly.

My eyes flutter closed again.

"Hey!" He shakes me.

I guess that's why my back's not touching the ground, it's because he is holding me up. He pulls me into his lap. I open my eyes but they roll around in my head unable to focus on anything.

I want to stay awake… but I'm so tired. It doesn't matter that I'm keeping my eyes open, everything in my vision is growing lighter and it's impossible to make out anything. I can't tell where one shape ends and another begins. The colors of the world around me are blending together. I miht as well close them, they're not doing me any good.

"No, no, no come on! We gotta get you up! Come on! Stay awake. You can't close your eyes yet. Stay awake. Come on!"

I feel him pulling me up, I wince and cry out. It hurts so bad.

"Come on, Soph. Stay with me."

It's strange. The last time this happened… when I felt my consciousness slipping away in the woods… the world sank into darkness. I didn't see anything or hear anything… but not this time. This time I feel as though I'm sinking into an odd glowing white abyss… it's comfortable. I kind of like it… so calm… peaceful…

"No, Sophie! Focus! You've got to stay conscious! Don't you pass out on me! Just hold on! Someone should be here real soon OK? You just gotta stay conscious 'til then! Alright?"

I try to make out his face, but it's too hard to tell him apart from the white fog of everything else that is in my vision. Am I even looking in the right direction?

"Just concentrate on my voice. I'm gonna keep talking, just stay with my voice. Don't let go! you've gotta concentrate, alright, just hold on…"

Kael keeps babbling on and on… I just want to rest… to relax in the white radiance… I don't want to have to fight the exhaustion anymore… I'm sorry…

"Sophie? Come on, no! Please don't! Please!" He sobs.

The whiteness brightens… I'm not cold anymore, but I am not particularly *warm,* per se, either… I'm just… I don't know… just… *nothing,* I guess. But it's a good nothing. I'm in a calm, peaceful, comfortable state of pure nothingness… and I don't care to do a thing about it.

White… abyss… of… satisfying… nothing…

29.

Departed

I stare at her blank eyes – she's not breathing anymore – I can see it. There's nothing there. I've seen this blankness many times in my 24 years but it's never felt anything like this. She's gone. That's what it means. She's gone.

"No!" I bawl. "No, no, no! Please no! Please! Soph! Come back! Please!"

I squeezed her tight, very aware of the giant shard of glass sticking through her chest. Tears stream down my face. This is all *his* fault! I look at my *brother* on the ground. *He* gets to live. Sophie is dead and *he* gets to live. How is that right? I glare at him, his outstretched hand twitches... he's holding something. What is that? A syringe. A syringe! A syringe full of blood! Could it be – yes it is! It has to be! His blood! Yes! Of course! I hadn't... GAH!

Quickly I reach for it trying not to disturb Sophie. I can't... reach!

"UGH!"

Inching myself closer, dragging her with me until I do finally reach it. I turn it over in my hand. It has to be! Quickly, I drag my forefinger and thumb over the needle to clean it off, and adjust Sophie's head.

"This is gonna work, Soph."

I stick the needle into her neck, empty it, pull it out, and toss it aside. Come on work!

Wrapping my arms around her again, I pull in her close.

I wait. Nothing. Come on Soph! Please!

"Sophie! Come on!"

She jolts and simultaneously takes a giant gulp of air like she just received CPR. I exhale a huge sigh of joy and relief.

"No... What..." She begins to hyperventilate.

"Hey, hey, calm down."

She sucks in another ragged breath of air.

"Get it out."

I immediately understand.

"I got it, I got it. Just – "

I lean her forward and grip the glass.

"Ahhh!" She winces.

"You alright?"

"Yeah, yeah, pull it out."

I yank it free and she inhales sharply through her teeth. Then she jumps to her feet holding the material of her shirt out of the way as she watches her skin seal itself back up. I get to my feet as well. She looks at me.

"What did you do?"

"I gave you his – "

She presses her palms to her temples. Eyes wide. She panicked. Why is she panicking?

"Why would you do that?" She shouts catching me off guard.

I grab her wrists and pull her hands away from her head.

"What are you talking about? You were dead!"

"I was?" Her eyes flood with a new emotion.

"Yes!"

"You shouldn't have given me that stuff. That's exactly what he wanted!"

She tries to yank her wrists out of my grasp but I'm not ready to let go yet. I just got her back.

"Hey! Stop! Just calm down," I tell her sternly

"He got what he wanted. I don't want to last forever with that! We can't be the last two – " She rambles.

"What?"

"We have to undo it somehow!" She goes on. "There has to be a way! You shouldn't have done – "

"Hey!" I cut her off. "We'll figure this out, OK? But I had to bring you back!"

She's silent, looking anywhere but me.

"Where is he?" She asks.

"What?"

I let go of her wrists and turn to look at where Gage went down. He's gone.

"No, no, no! That stuff should have knocked him out for hours!"

She drops her forehead into the tips of her fingers.

"Sedatives don't work on him," she sighs. "He was faking so he could take off. He manipulated that whole situation."

"Hey." I pull her hands away from her head so she'll look at me. "I'm gonna find him."

She smiles weakly holding my gaze.

"If you don't, I will."

"No, he's not going to get to you again." I promise, squeezing her hands reassuringly.

"That's not what I meant," she quips darkly.

"We'll figure this out, Soph."

I hold her. Listening to the chopper come in overhead and the squeal of tires. Reinforcements have arrived. 'Bout fucking time. I let go and look to the skies. The helicopter comes down, landing about twenty feet away. I put myself between *it* and *her*. DeWitt is the first to surface followed by three grunts with guns.

"What the hell happened?" DeWitt's angered voice cuts through the noise of the slowing propeller.

"You said she'd be safe!" I fume.

"Sophie – " He starts, but I don't want to hear another word out of his mouth.

"No! *You* don't talk to her! *You* talk to *me*! You have *no idea* what she's just been through! *I* do. *I* had to watch! You talk to *me*!"

Sophie is grabbing my arm and saying something but I don't know what. All I can hear in my head is *kill this motherfucker*. Fucking kill him right now.

"Kael!" Her voice breaks through the fog of rage.

DeWitt walks up to us.

"Sophie, is that your blood?" He asks urgently, picking up speed.

The image of her blank eyes flashes back into my head and I lose it.

"Kael!" Sophie shouts but it doesn't stop me from grabbing DeWitt's shirt and reeling him into a right hook to the face. He holds out his hand behind him to steady the approaching agents with guns.

"Is it hers?" I bellow. "Yeah it's hers!"

"Kael! Stop! Just wait a second!" Sophie orders.

I don't let go of DeWitt. But I take a breath. Hold it. Look at Sophie. And breathe as evenly as I can.

"This is too much." She presses her palms back into her temples. "Can you just stop! For five fucking minutes! Just stop."

I set free DeWitt's shirt. For her. He stumbles back and quickly composes himself. Wiping the blood under his nose with his sleeve, making room for the stream that's still coming out.

"Now then…" He fixes his shirt. "We're going to need to relocate as soon as we're able. I think the safest place for her right now is under your watch, with me and the rest of your colleagues.

30.

Partnerships

"**S**o how are you holding up?" Kael asks as he puts the car in park inn the middle of my driveway.

"It's weird 'cause I feel like I should be sore but I'm not – anywhere – at all. So your brother seems nice. And by nice, of course, I mean a real mother – "

"That was *not* Gage," Kael interjects. "I had a talk with DeWitt before I saw you earlier. He told me what was going on."

He pauses, turning off the car.

"They took a piece out of his brain. And what grew back is cold, dangerous and... merciless... I won't let them do that to you. *That* is why I was willing to *play nice*. Because I need to be *there*. In the *same room*."

I don't know how to respond to that.

"Alright." He reaches down and unclasps his seatbelt then turns to grab the door handle.

"Wait a minute – hold on. Where are you going?" I inquire as patronizingly as I can manage, pulling his shoulder, pressing him back against his seat.

He sighs, already exasperated.

"I'm coming with you. I'm not letting you out of my sight."

"You don't need to come; I'll be fine in there. I don't need a bodyguard for every second of my life. I'm *not* gonna be able to deal with that. Give me some normalcy, *please.*"

"Are you serious right n – "

"Kael," I blurt sternly. "I died today" I stare him down and I narrow my eyes. "I'm moving into your place for *who knows how long* with you and your *seven brothers*. I'm gonna need ten minutes to *myself* in *my house,* in *my room,* to collect some of *my stuff*, OK? You see what I'm getting at?"

He freezes for a couple seconds. Raises his hands in defeat as a smirk crosses his face. Then he drops his arms back to his sides, relaxes, and leans back in his seat.

"Ten minutes." He confirms. "A second more and I will assume something is wrong and break down the goddamn door, *capiche*?"

"Mhmm," I moan, adequately annoyed.

I turn and push open the door.

"Wait," his tone is desperate.

I stop and force myself to look at him, dreading what he might say after an introduction like that.

"Take this," he continues, digging in his pocket. He pulls out a knife... the knife I used to kill...

I stare at it. Paralyzed. I feel like... I can't speak.

"I think you should hold onto it. I think – " he sighs. "It'll help you come to terms with... you know... with how life's gonna be now. Because this thing... It ain't gonna end pretty. I know that now. I need you to be like me. I need you to be able to get through *this*. Because *I need you*."

He holds the knife out to me. I reach over and take it. I turn it over in my hand and flip it open. Then I flip it closed. I nod without looking at him.

Without a word, I get out of the vehicle and trek to the front door. I slide the knife into my back pocket, and grab the handle on the front door. Twist. Locked. *Well of course it's locked.* I forgot I don't have a key. Dropping my head I turn to look at the smugly expectant expression on the cocky lock-pickers face as he sits in the car waiting for me to wave him over. Pfft, yeah. Because that's something I'd do.

I roll my eyes locking them onto the second floor window that leads to the living room. It's cracked open. I walk to the flagpole hanging from the porch, pull it out, and walk back to the window. I press the end of the pole into the top of the screen and slide it up, then place it gently under the window, then slide that out of the way as well. I place the flagpole back in its holder and glance briefly at Kael's cocked eyebrow.

Quickly I climb up on the porch railing and pull myself up and through the window. I shut the screen and make my way to my room.

I can't die... I feel so strange right now.... I should do something crazy. Like learn how to ride a motorcycle... or a bull. Or, I don't know. The opportunities are endless. I could jump off a building just to say I did. Or see if punching a shark in the nose actually does scare it away... I can't go hide away in Kael's house. I've been given a rare opportunity to do a bunch of shit that would definitely kill me... and not die.

I walk down the hall and into my room, grabbing the door. I close myself in. Or rather, shut out the world. I rest my forehead on the door and exhale then turn around to lean against it. I hang my head giving myself a view of the floor before me as my hair partially curtains my face from the rest of the room. Yes. Eventually I have to do something about this. I can't live forever. But right now... I want to live the way people don't *get* to.

"Hey, gorgeous."

I convulse and wrench my hair back out of my face to locate the intruder. He's lounging on my bed with his arms crossed on his chest and his back propped up against the pillows.

"Looks like someone's had a rough day. Wanna talk about it?" Gage asks with a devilish smile.

I reach behind my back for the door handle not looking away from him.

I spin around opening the door within the motion, but I only make it a couple of inches through the door frame before I'm yanked back into the room by my hair. His arm snakes around my waist and I'm flying through the air until my back crashes against the wall beside the door.

He releases my waist as his other hand flies up to my neck to hold me firmly to the wall. I pry at his fingers like a madwoman, gouging at the flesh of my own neck to get between *it* and his hold, but it does me no good. He only squeezes tighter. I grab the knife out of my back pocket, flip it open, and plunge into his shoulder just beside his neck.

He's virtually unaffected. No wince. No nothing.

"Jesus," I utter.

He chuckles softly dropping his hands from my neck and placing them on his hips. I collapse to the floor caressing my neck trying to soothe it and breathe correctly. He looks at the floor and sniffs, then wipes his nose with his index finger as he looks up at the window. Kael's out there and he knows it.

"Tolerance, Sophie, is something I built up in that *hell*. But *you* – " He locks his gaze on me as he grips the knife and pulls slowly until it's free. "For *you*, I imagine this would hurt a *lot*. It'd be *excruciating*." His eyes darken. "Hasn't anyone told you it's *dangerous* to bring a knife to a fight you can't win?" He relaxes his knife wielding hand to his side.

"Yes, actually. Somewhat recently."

He chuckles admiringly.

"Haven't you done enough?" I continue, still choking to suck in air.

"Hey. Now, that's not fair." He whines theatrically. "*Kael's* the one who *did it*. Why does everything have to be *my* fault."

"*You* set it up," I retort, steadily raising my voice.

"Potato, potata," he sighs dismissively like I'm boring him. "Anyway, I didn't come here to split hairs."

"Why *are* you here?" I snap.

"To discuss our business arrangement."

"Business arrangement?"

"Yes. Because regardless of what you think of me," he waves the knife around, pointing it at me, "we're gonna need to help each other out if we wanna get anything done about our

211

predicament." He grabs the bottom of his shirt, pinches it over the bloody knife and rubs. "You can start off by not telling anyone we're in touch. I'd like to remain a silent partner for now. I could stand to be out of the spotlight for a while. You're gonna be my eyes in the blind spots. Keep me in the loop. Anything *you* learn, that *I don't* already know I'm gonna need you to share it."

"And why would I do any of that?"

"Because – My snarky little ally – I'm taking a trip down to Orlando, Florida to keep an eye on dear little Bruce, to make sure nothing happens to him while he's doin' that summer program."

"You son of a bitch!" I shout, already back on my feet.

"Jeez, Snarky. Relax." He cuts me off with his open palm outstretched. "I'm not gonna *do anything*. I told you, *I'm gonna make sure nothing happens to him*. You painted a big fat target on the back of that boy's head when you became relevant and – well, after all I can't use him *against you* if he's dead."

I narrow my eyes.

"You share. You keep your mouth shut. And I let Bruce continue to live." He clarifies. "And as far as selling me out, I understand you're not one to make *good* choices, but rather, *ballsy* ones. So let's get this straight, you cross me, and *I will be what happens to Bruce*. Let's see if you can do a better job than Kael at watching out for your little brother."

He moves the door out of his way but pauses to stare at me a little longer. I continue to glare at him.

"I'm not the bad guy, Soph. If you're smart, you'll figure that out for yourself *real soon.*"

I narrow my eyes further.

"See ya 'round, Snarky," he looks down at his occupied hand. "Nice knife."

He stabs the knife into the drywall and walks through the door, closing it behind him.

31790191R00124

Made in the USA
Middletown, DE
12 May 2016